THRU THE SMOKY END BOARDS

THRU THE SMOKY END BOARDS

CANADIAN POETRY ABOUT SPORTS & GAMES

Kevin Brooks & Sean Brooks, Editors

THRU THE SMOKY END BOARDS

Canadian Poetry About Sports & Games

This copyright page is continued in the Acknowledgements on page 236.

Polestar Book Publishers
1011 Commercial Drive, Second Floor
Vancouver, BC
Canada V5L 3X1
(604) 251-9718

The publisher would like to thank the Canada Council, the British Columbia Ministry of Small Business, Tourism and Culture, and the Department of Canadian Heritage for their ongoing financial assistance.

Cover painting by Jennifer Ettinger
Cover design by Jim Brennan
Printed and bound in Canada

CANADIAN CATALOGUING IN PUBLICATION DATA
Main entry under title:
Thru the smoky end boards

ISBN 1-896095-15-1
1. Sports—Poetry. 2. Canadian poetry (English)—20th century.
I. Brooks, Kevin, 1968- II. Brooks, Sean, 1966- III. Title:
Through the smokey end boards.
PS8287.S59T78 1996 C811'.508'0355 C96-910008-6
PR9195.85.S59T78 1996

FOR LAURA, PATTI AND KAELEN

Acknowledgements

This book was a family effort. Sean and I collaborated for over a year on this project, although we saw each other only once during that time. Our mom, Beth Brooks, entered most of the poems while visiting us (neither of us are half the typist she is), and our dad, Alf Brooks, proofread and provided valuable feedback.

Thank you to everyone who has shown interest in, and given encouragement to, this project. Early support came from members of the Sports Literature Association and Birk Sproxton. Friends in Iowa and Vancouver kept us excited about the book when we started to feel overwhelmed — special thanks go to Cory McClure and Mike of Sportsbook Plus. Nancy Blyler and Guy Robertson provided us with advice as teachers and friends. Chris Hicks was a valuable reader and turned up some great poems, and Michelle Benjamin of Polestar made many wonderful contributions to this book as editor and poem-finder. Graham Freeman told us about "The Bonspiel Song."

The authors of these poems deserve the credit for the strengths of this book, and we thank them for their permission to have their work reprinted here.

CONTENTS

BASEBALL

Canadian Poetry about Sports & Games

> *What this fan is missing most of all is the poetry, the subtle ebb and flow of the game, its fluidity, range, and patterns.*
> *Doug Beardsley,* Country on Ice

In Al Purdy's "Hockey Players," bored fans sit in the blues until three players "break down the ice in roaring feverish speed." The fans explode out of their seats and selves, joining the players as they skate "thru the smoky end boards," climb up Appalachian Highlands, cross the Laurentian Barrens, skate over Hudson's Bay, and out onto the treeless tundra. Skating, swimming, running, climbing or simply playing thru the smoky end boards, thru mysterious and arbitrary boundaries, is a striking image of our bodies and imaginations in motion. This collection brings together a wide range of poems that capture and release the spirit of endless, imaginative play whether in hockey, skating, baseball, swimming, golf or the many other sports and games Canadians play and watch. *Thru the Smoky End Boards* is a collection of poems for the fan and player who want to re-live, re-imagine, or re-examine the joy and the terror of playing. It is a book for the fan, like Doug Beardsley, who has been missing the poetry of sports and games.

Sports and games swim with classic and modern themes of literature. The celebration and the tragedy of the hero, anti-heroism — or what might be seen as the celebration and tragedy of the average player — and the complicated relationship between gender and sports are three important themes in this book. But before exploring those themes, we will start with the tricky issue of defining something uniquely Canadian about these poems.

The presence of Rocket Richard, Gordie Howe, Wayne Gretzky, Bobby Orr, Bobby Hull, Manon Rhéaume, Don Cherry, Bill Barilko, Howie Morenz, Emily Carr, George Young, Maggie T[rudeau], and the Hamilton Tigercats may be the clearest evidence for saying that these poems are distinctly Canadian. Stew Clayton's country and western tune, "The Bonspiel Song," could *only* be a product of Canada. But the deeper question about Canadian poetry is whether or not there is a Canadian experience, a Canadian point of view, expressible in words. The many poems about the lone figure — not an individual triumphing against the odds but a humble athlete, frightened by the awesome wilderness, as in Charles G.D. Roberts' "The Skater" — express a strong element of the Canadian psyche. But the easy mingling of sporting heroes and their fans in Raymond Souster's "Christmas-Morning Hockey" also suggests the sense of community one finds within Canada and among

Canadians around the globe. The strong sense of being first and foremost an individual, yet always a part of a community, may be the uniquely Canadian theme of *Thru the Smoky End Boards.*

Another important element of Canadian self-definition is the degree to which we define ourselves as "not Americans." Canadians, as Purdy notes in his hockey poems, are constantly trying to overcome an "anguish of inferiority" when measuring up against Americans. The Canadian poets represented here match up well against their American counterparts, even when taking up the American game. George Bowering, Judith Fitzgerald, Ken Norris, and Raymond Souster write baseball poetry as insightful, magical, and tragic as the poetry of John Updike, Marianne Moore, Donald Hall, and Robert Francis. The excesses of American sporting culture are ridiculed in Florence McNeil's "Half Time Parade," and the pain of losing a Canadian hero to Hollywood is recorded in John B. Lee's "The Trade that Shook the Hockey World." "[M]y nation trembled," Lee writes about the Gretzky trade, for all sorts of difficult-to-articulate reasons, the last of which seems most profound to him: "something about moving too fast in time." The trading and selling of Canada to the U.S. has moved so quickly through Canada's short history that not until Canada loses such an important symbol as Wayne Gretzky is the impact really felt.

Souster goes back in time, as if attempting to repair, or deny, the American impact and influence on Canada. He suggests that the American invasion of Toronto in 1813 was finally given a proper retort when the "Jays Win American League East, 1985" in a victory over the Yankees. Like the problem of being an individual in a community, Canada and Canadian poetry seems *like* America and American poetry, yet can be identified as *not* American. At best, we can say that this collection of poems will not define what it means to be Canadian, nor even what Canadian poetry or the Canadian sporting experience is. But *Thru the Smoky End Boards* will illuminate some of the similar ways Canadians think about their games, their heroes, and their nation.

The celebration of Canadian sports heroes, like Lee's poem on the Gretzky trade, is more often than not mixed with elements of tragedy. Souster attributes our shallow treatment of heroes to our fickleness as he notes the rise to fame and the fall to obscurity of oarsman Ned Hanlan in "Our Boy in Blue." But Souster also seems to suggest that heroes eventually will be properly rewarded: a statue for Hanlan was erected after his death. Purdy and Don Gutteridge celebrate the brilliance and fire of Rocket Richard, but Purdy sees in "Homage to Ree-shard" that brilliance is closely allied with madness, and Gutteridge ends "Arena" not with hope but with an image of the player's and the poet's imagination collapsed "in Roman ruin." Richard Harrison sees the weight of heroism "flooding [Gretzky's] limbs beyond bearing" in "On the American Express Ad Photo of Cardmembers Gordie Howe and Wayne Gretzky Talking After the Game."

The passing of time ensures that heroism and excellence will always be short-lived, always mixed with tragedy and decline. Ken Norris tries to preserve the brilliance of Andre Dawson, even as "The Hawk" slumps near the end of his career, and Alix Vance both celebrates the youthful brilliance and mourns the death of "The Diamond Warrior," Ab Ettinger. The biggest names in sport like Dawson and the local heroes like Ettinger suffer the same fate. R. G. Everson's poem for Canadian swimming great George Young may be one of the few celebrations of heroism that does not mix success and tragedy because Everson celebrates Young's character, a life-long quality, rather than his fleeting athletic ability.

The anti-hero is as prevalent in sports poetry as is the hero. Poets often poke fun at their own athletic limitations, making poetry from their least poetic moments. Stephen Scriver, ironically self-titled the All-Star Poet, exemplifies the anti-hero. His books are most readily found at gas stations in Saskatchewan, and their subject is often the indignity of sports. "Once is Once Too Many" combines a non-poetic title with the non-heroic act of painfully scoring via a "three-ball combination" while not wearing a protective cup. The anti-hero, however, is not found in farce alone. John B. Lee's collection *The Hockey Player Sonnets* has many fine poems about the average or below-average player still enjoying the game, best represented in this collection by "Industrial League Hockey." A recurring image for George Bowering is hitting a bases-loaded single after being a fringe player for years, only to have to give up the game after his most heroic act. Leona Gom's anti-hero feels out of place in the world of aerobics, struggling to fit in, struggling to feel superior to "The Class Junkie," but ultimately failing in the fight to keep off extra pounds.

Gom's other contribution to this collection, "Sport," might be called an "anti-fan" poem, but the issue she raises goes further than simply not understanding sports. She sees a strange arrangement of gender roles: "even the man who will / do your seediest laundry, who is / a better mother than you are, will / turn surly when you laugh about hockey." The issue is not simply that men inexplicably like sports and women do not, but that sports are so thoroughly gendered as masculine that some athletes and fans are uncomfortable with the roles they assume when they take up sports and games. Gom cannot understand how this man is both so traditional and so modern. Mark Cochrane writes of his "fear of shower-rooms & locker chat" and being a traitor to manhood in "Boy." Cochrane also addresses the very issue that Gom and Roo Borson in "Hockey Night in Canada" raise: sports' ability to transform its watchers, most of whom are men, and to distract them from their relationships with the people around them. Cochrane's persona shows considerable remorse in "Tear Gas" for neglecting his family in order to watch hockey while on vacation, yet he could not resist the lure of the game. Richard Harrison notes the "want of the truly feminine" in hockey and seems to understand why so few women would want to watch. He also deplores the fact that Manon Rhéaume cannot be respected as a player: "we do not forget that she is always a woman and sex is everything."

Sex, or gender, does seem to be everything. Judith Fitzgerald's "The Baseball Hall of Fame" tells the story of a young woman crazy about baseball: "She always wanted to play baseball / but baseball had a heart of its own." Giving up baseball for domestication proved to be an "uneasy alliance" at best. Kate Braid is also made uneasy by her son's translation of "making connection." When Braid suggests to her lacrosse-goalie son that he imagine himself as a tree deeply rooted in the earth as a strategy for overcoming nervousness, he responds that he does have a similar strategy: hitting someone or yelling at the ref. "This is what boys do," he says. His mom can't understand, however, because girls do things differently.

Gail Harris, in contrast, is not puzzled by the relationship between chauvinist attitudes and sports. She suggests the Indianapolis Speedway and a special fourteen-hole golf course in Miami for "Jerks" are among the places that these sporting men can be found. Erin Mouré's questions about sports go beyond questions about gender and relationships. "A Sporting Life" and "Palm Sunday" suggest the ability of pastimes to blind a whole culture to events as monumental as the second coming of Christ or as reprehensible as sexual assault.

Of course, not all women who write on sports overtly address gender issues. Margaret Atwood's contributions, "Younger Sister, Going Swimming" and "Woman Skating," and Susan Ioannou's "Golf Lesson," are portraits of the strength, beauty, and potential of bodies in motion. Dorothy Livesay attempts to trace the movement of the ball as poetry in "Soccer," and Margaret Avison celebrates "Tennis:" "Service is joy, to see or swing." Poems about the female athlete, however, are never far from questioning the gender roles of our society. Lorna Crozier's "The Swimmer" moves from a celebration of grace, strength, and motion, to questions: "If she climbs from the pool / will she become an ordinary woman [?]" The poets in *Thru the Smoky End Boards* do not seem to be suggesting that sex differences are essential — that there is something defineably male and something defineably female. They seem worried, pissed off, or overwhelmed by the fact that these patterns of masculine and feminine qualities and actions continue to repeat themselves, and often through sports. When sports do offer consolation, that consolation is in the form of an escape rather than solution.

Thru the Smoky End Boards is not, ultimately, a celebration of the hero or a critique of our sporting culture, but a book that contains many poetic visions of sporting experiences. We included the majority of poems we found relating to sport, although we had to select from some of the complete works on hockey: Harrison's *The Hero of the Play*, Lee's *The Hockey Player Sonnets*, Scriver's *More All-Star Poet*, and Birk Sproxton's prose poetry *The Hockey Fan Came Riding*. Bowering and Souster, both well represented here, have many other poems on sports and games that could be collected. The poems we have selected represent both early and late works in these two poets' careers and, for Souster, they represent many, though not all, of the sports about which he has written.

John Frederic Herbin's "The Diver" (1899) is the oldest poem reprinted here, and a handful of poems by Mark Cochrane are being published for the first time: "99," "Dancing on the Machine," "High Five," "Tear Gas" and "The Speed of Falling Bodies." Some of the poems were familiar to us when we started the project; many more were found by sifting through anthologies, individual collections of poetry, and journals. Others still were mentioned to us by friends. We decided not to include poems about hunting and fishing, partly because of thematic dissonance, but largely because such poems are so numerous they could form a volume of their own. The one thing we are certain of is that we have not exhausted the scope of Canadian poetry on sports and games. Whether as central subject, illuminating metaphor, or key allusion, acts of playing are consistently powerful images for poets.

For some readers, Earle Birney's "David" and Margaret Atwood's "Circle Game" might be two conspicuous absences from this collection. Birney's interest in climbing is represented by "Climbers," and we have chosen to let the familiarity of "David" speak for itself. However, readers might think of Mark Cochrane's "Three Years From Long Beach" as a poem that responds to and deals with some of the same issues as Birney's "David." The metaphor of "game" that Atwood makes central to "Circle Game" is well represented in the final section of *Thru the Smoky End Boards* by Saint-Denys-Garneau's "The Game," Douglas Lochead's "The Game," Rhona McAdam's "Circle Game," and Florence McNeil's "A Game." For those who have not encountered either Atwood or Birney, their works are widely published, and both poems are frequently anthologized.

Hockey's status in Canadian culture and the prevalence of Canadian hockey poems justifies their pole position in this collection. Baseball is the next most written about sport in Canadian poetry, and provides a sharp contrast to hockey as both the summer and the American game.

The groupings after *Hockey* and *Baseball* push at the limits of organization. The poems about golf, although found in the *In Competition* section, are almost evenly split between poems that see golfers, as Irving Layton does, as "metaphysicians," and those that see golfers, as E. J. Pratt does, as "Jocks." Team sports and sports that involve scoring or clear winners became the defining line for inclusion in *In Competition*, even though all poems in that section do not involve the motif of competition. Some *Lone Figures*, by contrast, are deeply involved in competition, or like Maggie T, are simply "going public." But on the whole, swimmers, skaters, runners, climbers, and the other athletes collected in this section often spend considerable time alone. The final section, *A Sporting Life*, draws its title from Erin Mouré's poem grouped with the soccer poems. *A Sporting Life* continues the theme of Mouré's poem; this section contains poems about obsessive exercising and life itself becoming a game. While *A Sporting Life* may seem to be a catch-all — an open league for anyone who has mentioned playing, games, or sports — works like Michael Ondaatje's "To a Sad Daughter" and Bronwen Wallace's "Green Light, Red Light" are among the most powerful poems in *Thru the Smoky End Boards*.

Within these groupings, poets and poems have been organized alphabetically except where a particular sequence held a narrative line or a chronological development. Organizing poems by sport rather than by author disturbs the thematic relationship of connected works like C. H. Gervais' Maggie T poems, but emphasizes the themes and issues that particular sports generate. Reading by author rather than sport would be a way to play with the format of *Thru the Smoky End Boards*, and would enact the playfulness about which so many of these poets write.

The one great theme of this book that can *almost* go without mentioning is the close relationship between art and play. Robert Kroetsch's poetic account of Howie Morenz and Emily Carr's marriage in many ways sums up this theme. Morenz and Carr's marriage is one that at first seems highly improbable, but upon further contemplation, is seen to be a perfect match: "The hockey player, the artist: they both have / strong wrists." This book is the product of that marriage, a marriage that continues to grow stronger.

HOCKEY

That night I would dream for the first time
of the goaltender ...

— Mark Cochrane

Gordie and My Old Man

When I first met Gordie
I was seventeen.
Dad called him a hoodlum
in tight blue jeans
but Dad he ain't like
you'd ever be.
He's fast, and he's sharp
and he's wild about me.
Well, it's been three kids
in seven years.
Gordie works with Dad
hauling cases of beer
and I ain't as shapely
as I used to be
but I like Gordie
and he likes me.
Gordie and my old man
on a Saturday night
watching the Blackhawks
and getting tight.
Nothing ever changes
in this world of mine
it's Gordie and my old man
on a Saturday night.
He never takes me dancing
'cause he's slow on his feet
but he's good with the kids
through the rest of the week
and on Saturday nights
you know where I'll be
with Gordie and my old man
and that old tv
I remember being a little girl
watching Dad swear
when the frenchmen scored.
The circle keeps moving
but it never seems to change
'cause here comes Montreal
on a breakaway.

ROO BORSON

Hockey Night in Canada

In the blue light at the far end of the darkened house,
shadowy players shoot and score,
continual apocalypse in the announcer's voice.
My companion, lost to it,
dark negative of the self,
one silhouetted foot jutting into the near light of the TV.
Distanced roar of speed and heroics,
the miniaturized raging and cheering.
Now and then against the quiet of the house
his wild dissension, little world,
and the cat moves like a lament,
its wants not the usual ones,
not usual and so
indefinite, unmet.

At the arena

there is
fluorescence
stale popcorn
wood   scarred by skate blades   healed by falling beer
it's so ugly and cold and
familiar

the guys
horning their lust and rage
offer smokes to the snow maidens
cold-eyed at seventeen
who smile   hiding their teeth
and turn back to the game

the screams cut the lutheran air

when everyone leaves
even the Zamboni man
when the unforgiving lights are finally down
and the ice is again virginal

skate out in the vaulting
dark

race and turn
like the great ones

the rafters reverberate with
your name
unassisted

the scoreboard shows
that Home has finally won

MARK COCHRANE

Boy

Cathy says
You are always using the word
but I wonder what it means for you.

Richard says
This is my hockey. Did you ever see me play it?

I say
I hate the Father, but I love my dad.

Desperate for something but relieved at nothing
I bowed my head, I waited & waited
for a crop of hair, dark nimbus
to appear
& blot the white
chub of the pubis.

It was the one page I could not write, by will.

At twelve I quit the city "A" league
when smaller boys
with their compact torsion
began to lay me flat. I was big
but soft, sweat not pungent, not yet musk,
& worst of all
I was glad for that.

Trace to this moment, if you must,
my fear of shower-rooms & locker chat.

O pupae, O the smooth & featureless.
Grown men, the emissions of their skins,
revulsed me, & like (& unlike) a girl too thin
& wanting to be thinner, breastless, I dreaded
metamorphosis.

Every story of the adulthood of my body
begins the year I quit hockey clean, without muscle, &

when puberty finally came, I was fourteen,
it was too late. Manhood already knew
I was a traitor to its form.

But desire doubles back on disgust.

Now I'm back in the game with other men
& can hardly tell repulsion, or jealousy, from lust.

The homoerotic? I consume the other man in mind
to become him, sculpted & buffed
to a sheen, my ideal self in the imagined
eyes of women. (Oh, that's one disavowal …

O Daddy, O Daedalus, O magician:
because I could never measure up to your body
or your idea of it, brute & heavy
but perfectible, tight, & sexed for flight,

because I could never harden myself
to the sleekness of a rooster & rise,

I nearly drowned in a refusal
of the wings you had invented, I nearly proved
that the impressionable son
melts.

My dad, in the autumn of his seventeenth year,
was on the cusp of making
the major-junior team in Moose Jaw

(& everything that promised)

when he took a football cleat in the calf
& lost the season of both sports.

Where I come from
athletics are a man's first career.
Any other life
is a rebellion or a compromise
based on the failure to make pro.

Yesterday in the community centre
I stepped onto the rink, ice
wet & bluish
like the white of an eye
after the Zamboni run.

That smell, *air of the ice*, it hit me

like a shoulder to the lungs:

I am six years old & taking a face-off

at five-thirty in the morning, my dad
is a bushy bear
with seventies hair
& his moustache in the steam —

he is smiling over coffee —

a warm
rush of reassurance
from his cupped hands of prayer
in the stands.

This spring, after many apart, we attend
NHL games
like devotions, the arcana
& arithmetic of the sportspage
a way of talking.

As fathers, as dads, we are beginning
to find a way back, through men
& their measures,
to the meaning of a boy
& the soft, muscular care
he was born to.

MARK COCHRANE

Daddy is a Monkey

quips my son, gap-toothed
from his fall on the ice, a whole person
glistering from his eyes
to mine, hiccuping

giggles at his own joke,
just two-&-a-half
with a toy chimp stuffed
into a helmet & jersey
& playing in the slot

between his grandpa — my father — & me
on the sofa, as we dangle
from the final seconds
of the Kings' game, an arena
where we can meet, Dad reaching out
across space
& *his* father's pocket-watch, arranged
like a trophy on the hutch,
to caress my arm —

an awkward
animal grooming
in the glade of his apartment,
neither of us possessing
speech for this —

his opposable thumb in the hair
above my wrist
where the blood warms,
soothed & confused by the same touch
that tended me
when i was the boy who loved him
full in the face,
as a child will allow
for only so long: full
& unmasked, without a helmet
painted with a crown, & free
from the dread of any loss, sudden
or slow, even
as the clock was running down.

High Five

for Richard Harrison, 06/01/94

And then arms, all I can see is the arms of men, launched
by reflex, the fisted heads of a hundred Jacks
in the Box, that one second of event on the big screen
(invisible now) a flick of the collective trigger
& I rise to slap the naked palm in salute
of one I've never met, thumb cocked
behind his ear & creamy
ale in his other knuckles
sloshing over the pint-mug's lip

onto his jeans, he is laughing now with glassy
unvisored eyes into my face
& I am laughing the same face
back at him, as if *we* did it, as if me, this guy & his buddy
just bagged the goal in OT ourselves.

In the clank & bristle
he hugs his buddy's T-shirt, oh, brushcut & triceps, so
I turn back to my friends, still yelling as we strut
through double doors into the night air,
hoarse & jubilant, intimate, of course
I was thinking of you then, wishing you with us,
the phantom sting of a stranger's hand
still hot on the pads of my fingers.

That night I would dream for the first time
of the goaltender with a mask striped like a tiger.
He stands up in the rushes, stoical, & he pounces
with feline muscle. Seeing but not seen, with claws
laced tighter than a lover's into the stitching of his glove,
he reaches out to his fullest stretch for anything, for anyone,
& catches it, & squeezes, & holds on.

Tear Gas

The seventh game I watch on a fourteen-inch screen
beside Rathtrevor Bay, a hundred km from the Coliseum,
my daughter cradled between my legs with her rattles
& teethers on the cabin floor. So many family vacations
wounded by a city's unguessible ceremonies of June. My son
lumbers across the boards, addresses me in the voice
of a plastic orca in his hand. I deke him. Daddy
is watching now, I say, as if, wait — Pavel Bure
spits white between his watermelon lips
from the will-be losers' muster, & when I turn back
after a head fake — my son is gone, crying into his mother's shape
by a picnic table on the porch: benched.

This is Canada's game. Red-eyed, broken, sobbing
in MSG, shuddering up a manly breath
for post-game reporters. The Canucks tearful on tv,
my kids wailing, what a waste of pathos, what a shame
the father I become, looking for myself
in this spectacle:
WE ARE REFLECTED IN ALL WE SEE
spray-painted on the boarded shops, the broken teeth
of windows in downtown Vancouver
after the riots & the news, the corner of Robson & Thurlow
like a James Cameron film, hazy & gunmetal blue,
where troopers with masks & plastic shields also watch
as angry fans kick the canisters back.
At the cabin, logged
in, my son calls out my title in the night: *I thought
you went away, Dad-d-dy,* he stutters
against my face. Fog is rising
across the Strait & seeps
up the beach, through windows & cedar joints
like the vapours off dry ice. I whisper
to his sleep, roll with each squall, & his salt eyes
burn my cheek.

99

Speed, force of weapon, musculature:
there sleep armies of men who possess these
in bruter proportion — knight, bishop

& rook. On the grid of his mind glitters
an optic calculus. A triangulation
of the probable. He views each square

yet circles beyond rank, & without opposite.
Even the master who would be his mirror,
his nemesis to the sixes, reads only

bad oracles. Despair. No logic & no art
honed on the ice by flat-earthers
can foil a wizard who is arranging the stars.

Arena

for Maurice Richard

For the fifteen seasons
of my boyhood
I watched you
in that arena contained
by the TV screen
and the restless cameras
and yet made grander
by them
(like the forests to the north
of our village, with wolves,
like the prairies out West
bristling with Indians
or like the Lake beside us
wider than sea and more salty)
made it grander than our
home-built local rink,
and you, Maurice Richard,
outdistancing
                cameras
                focus
                Maple Leafs
                imagination
carrying my boyhood
on blades
farther than it deserved,
beyond the range
of ice

And when you fell
and your five hundred goals
about you
and the Forum diminished,
I was with you
when the ice gave way
in broken perfect circles,
when the marble timbers
and columns
of our mutual imagination
collapsed
          in Roman ruin.

DON GUTTERIDGE

Shooting

On mid-winter Saturdays
Jerry and I
took turns
                    shooting
our bodies
hungry   come from
thin beds to
open morning
and wide light

(by the walk
fresh dog-dirt
on the tired snow
bright as
rubbed pennies
in the after-
breakfast sun)

and Jerry and I
                    shooting
the joint-muscle
of arm and stick
flung
the long-arc'd puck
toward the goal,
my eye leaning
and longing   it
bit the backboards
with a rubber crunch
and wood made a
kind of grunt
I could feel
all the way down
to my balls,

and Jerry
doing the splits
and grinning because
his net had clung
to innocence
but mostly because
it was morning
and Saturday
for both of us,
and once
we paused to
watch two dogs

"doing it" by the walk,
the old fellow
pressing his eyeballs shut
and back down his throat
till I thought
he would shoot them like
two gaping icicles
straight and smoking
ice up her rear-end
                    bending
and bouncing
shot full of
morning down the street
heading (I believe)
with the breakfast
sun sniffing after her
— together —
            toward
                  lunch.

RICHARD HARRISON

The African Hockey Poems

1

When the manager of the gallery in the Hôtel
Ivoire sees the flag on my pack, he tells me he
loves my country and he plays hockey on the rink
that lies chilled like a pie in the middle of the hotel
on the equator where leaves rot as they grow and
the air is sweet as apples with their dying. I say
What position? He says *Left Wing*. I say *Like*
Bobby Hull. And Bobby's name makes it: he draws
his hand up and it smiles at the end of his arm:
this is The Shake, the one that begins with the slap
of palm against palm, the one between men
who've found enough between them to confirm
the world for a day and go on. Tomorrow I will
skate on this rink like the pros back home, way
ahead of schedule and nature; I will tell you
I touched the ice and I could be any boy in love.

2

For the photo shoot on the only rink in the Côte
d'Ivoire, I carry a hockey stick from the Canadian
Embassy through the streets of Abidjan, and the
stares of the passersby say no one knows what it is
just as the inland farmers who had never seen the
sea stared at Ulysses with his oar. The old king
waited for those stares, the oar become a butter
churn, a plough, the village speaker's staff when
the business of the day gives way to night. It is
time for the story to be told.

Coach's Corner

The almost clerical collar, he is the priest of rock 'em sock 'em. He silences his more knowledgeable friends with his faith in the bodies of men and without him and his kind the NHL would be vapid as the All-Star Game forever. He is loud and whiny and complaining and chokes up on air if he's hurt by someone's words — everything a man should not be, yet every sports bar wills itself to quiet, turns up the volume on its dozen sets only for his words. He is their man in a way no hero of the play could be; his big league career was a single game, but remember, he used to tell Bobby Orr what to do and Bobby listened as we listen though we let the game go on in silence. He slams foreigners, praises women in all the ways wrong for our time, rejects any wavering in the masculinity of his troops like a colonel in the US Marines. And yet he is here because he is unafraid to love, love the game, the journeyman players, love the code that makes a man a man and if you don't know, I ain't gonna tell ya. He loves the fans, for all the pain they cause him, and we are here with our own uncomfortable backs for that dogged love, the voice that rises like a tenor sax, pointed fingers, eyes narrowed to see clear and deep the world that has him trapped on two sides already.

The Feminine

My plan for a deck of hockey Tarot cards failed for want of the truly feminine. I could make some figure a woman in the game; Canada's women's team is the best in the world, and maybe I could push the notion until it does not matter, woman or man — just The Player. But I'd be lying. This is not why I love the game, or why its symbols work like runes in my language. This is a game the women watch, its gentler moments taken in their image: The Trainer, running to the Fallen Man Beside the Boards, cradling the face now loose and looking skyward in his hands, smoothing his hair with a towel; the Equipment itself, stockings, girdles, garters. At the time I did not understand what the woman next to me at a hockey game was trying to teach when she wondered aloud whether she would find a better lover in another woman as the players below us skated the warm-up, around and around their own side of Centre, lofting long, lazy Pucks at their Goalie. There is a Mask on my face, the game divides us. Again I've come to a profession of love in words I cannot use for you, with all the women left in the stands where I demand that you sit and love it all.

On the American Express Ad Photo of Cardmembers Gordie Howe and Wayne Gretzky Talking After the Game

The old man holds his hands in the middle air before him, raised and loose, explaining something only he and the kid who took his place in the record book even understand as a question. Hockey looks simple and fast the way Sumo looks simple and fast, and there are 78 named moves in Sumo though a match is over in 9 seconds or less, the time it takes a man to score a goal and the two who get assists to set him up. Advice is briefly spoken, takes years to hear; Gordie said to Wayne, *Work on your backhand.* Later Gretzky's father will lie dying in a Hamilton hospital and Wayne will take a check from behind into the boards. By reflex, he will take off his helmet, his heavy gloves, undressing himself on the ice in his pain, his own armour too heavy for his shocked skin. Unprotected, brought low, he will look the way he doesn't think he looks here, in this photo, receiving Gordie's wisdom, the weight of the game flooding his limbs beyond bearing.

Rhéaume

Here is the desire of Manon Rhéaume: to stop
the puck. Come down from the stands, strap on
the big pads, painted mask, disappear into *goalie*
the way a man can be a man and not a man
inside the armour. To forget in the motion of the
save that we do not forget she is always a
woman and sex is everything: if she wasn't pretty
she'd never hear her looks got her on the NHL
team in Tampa Bay where the ushers are women
hired from a bar called *Hooters*, and David
Letterman wouldn't have her on *Late Night*
prodding her again and again, *Say Ock-ee*; if
Brett Hull was ugly as a wet owl and scored 86
goals a season, still there'd be kids with his
poster on their bedroom doors. To be a woman
and have it be her play that counts. To stop the
puck where the best are men, for men to be
better than they are. On your wall is a collage of
women with their arms raised, they are dancing,
they are lifting weights, they are marching
against apartheid. One is a goddess with snakes
in her hands; Catwoman reaches for Gotham,
Boadicea shakes a spear in the face of Rome,
two nuns run splashing into the laughing waves:
here, I give you Rhéaume and a glove save, the
puck heading for the top corner. Stopped.

DAVID HELWIG

Stopping on Ice

Suddenly
he was down —
his eyes strange, someone said,
mouth open —
42 years old
coming back once a year
to the boys' game
for charity,
a red-faced man with children
and a job and a mortgage.

In 1949
he spent a playoff in the NHL
and that was as far as he got
in hockey
but he died on the ice, seen
by 2000 people
each one
catching a different angle
a different moment,
their eyes drawn away from the puck
converging like rays of light
on the broken moment
of his falling
2000 images
laid
one on top the other so that
I see him falling
over and over
going down in slow
motion
his face
like the boy's face
in tomorrow's newspaper, an Old Timer
playing for charity
passing the goal
reaching for the post
missing
coasting
on out near the blue line
sinking
to his knees
and reaching out
and falling —
4000 eyes
seeing a boy who had his kidney

pierced by a skate at sixteen —
                                        the red face
of the man darkening, sinking, gone now
as he fell to the silver ice
                                   slowly
2000 times
            like a boy
falling
        and dying.

LIONEL KEARNS

Hockey is Zen

Momentary satori as Frank
takes the pass on the right wing
fakes a shot to deek the defenceman
and fires the puck
into the lower lefthand corner
of the net, the whole play
so quick I would have missed it
if I'd blinked an eye

Frank handles his hockey stick
like a delicate instrument, a perfect
extension of physical self
and I, sitting high above the ice
think of a Samurai swordsman:
elegance and exact precision
the gestures executed
in a flash of instant decision

Frank rarely smiles when thinking
about hockey, and is sometimes
troubled after the game
by the memory of a wrong move
But on the ice his skates
dance and cut patterns that are
the intricate and perfectly realized
choreography of a mind
honed and polished by the action
of immediate response

Listening to the Radio: For Michael Ondaatje

Morenz makes a breakaway down the ice.
He fakes to the left; he draws out the goalie.
He stops. He blushes and says, to all
of the Montreal Forum: Emily Carr, I love you.

Everyone is surprised. The puck delays
the stick, only the ice moves. The (almost)
invisible moment, before he (Morenz) shoots.
The goalie's mask in the goal's mouth.

The splendid rigour of his pads. Not the puck
in the net but the goalie's mask, moving
and stopping. Emily thinks of berry-picking.
She wants to sit in the penalty box.

If you eat the berries, she thinks, the pail
will never fill. Pay attention to the play,
Howie, she whispers, across the blue line.

Everyone is surprised. She blushes and says,
The wedding will be divided into three periods
of twenty minutes each. Morenz shoots.

Reading It in the (Comic) Papers: For bp

In a delightful ceremony at the bride's
boarding house in Victoria, the nuptial
event is consummated. The family
of Mr. Morenz is not in attendance.

Among the highlights of the afternoon
is the arrival of the poet bpNichol of Toronto
in the company of Mr. Basho of Japan,
the latter using a hockey stick as his staff.

Work on your line, bp quips (he is wearing
his Buddha shirt) when introduced to the
famous hockey player by Miss Carr (who will retain
her maiden name). Keep it edgy,

Mr. Morenz replies, scoring a point
of his own while he takes the hockey stick
from Mr. Basho's hand — that same Mr. Basho
offering, in his now empty hands, his gift:

When we both talk, Mr. Basho says, speaking
to all those present, the words are listening.

The Bridegroom Rises to Speak

At the wedding reception, such as it is,
Howie Morenz is asked to say a few words.
He is about to oblige when a menagerist
enters the parlour, accompanied by thirteen

ghazals. I thought ghazals were animals,
Howie says, into the microphone. He gives himself
a body check. He doesn't much like the wedding cake,
he's having a slice of Limburger cheese with onion.

Howie feels about Limburger cheese the way Emily
feels about monkeys. A matter of parallel lines
that meet. The mathematics of (pure) desire.
The hockey player, the artist: they both have

strong wrists. Perhaps, says Emily, the salmon,
coming back, wish to climb the totem tree, or
time is the monkey, descending. Or, Mr. Basho
continues, it is simply a matter of setting out

when you are old. He walks across the parlour
and mingles with the ghazals. Howie takes a bow.

Wedding Dance, Country-Style

This will not be, Mr. Ondaatje explains,
your standard epithalamium. He is taking
pictures, both in colour and black and white.
The bride and the bridegroom are dancing.

Actually, everyone is dancing. George
(which George?) is dancing, with Gertrude Stein.
All of Victoria, later, expresses embarrassment,
but the dance, the dance is full of marvels.

Roy Kiyooka arrives by balloon. He drops in
for a polka. He is the only person who brings
an escape plan as a gift. It is a collage
of 1,243 pages, in code, with maps and diagrams,

all of which Mr. Ondaatje photographs
as part of the epithalamium, and the ecstatic
document, in arrest, has about it the air

of a painting of a forest exploding into light,
or of a hockey game, under the lights, exploding.
But the dance, the dance is the first decoding.

Philosophy of Composition: For Paul Thompson

The shivaree is pronounced a success,
taking place as it does near the family home
of the bridegroom; the assembled neighbours,
who start the evening in disgruntlement, sing

the couple's praise, then eat pancakes at dawn,
with maple syrup, to the music of gun and kettle,
thanks to the magical red cape and skills
theatrical of Mr. Thompson, an oldish young man

who as a boy in southwestern Ontario played road
hockey with Howie Morenz, the two of them (players)
knocking frozen horse turds up and down an otherwise
quiet street and, in the process, recognizing

as had the bride, Miss Carr, earlier, while being
violently seasick in a small boat that was
(supposedly) carrying her to a site where she might
make sketches and, fortunately, sit reasonably still

that the cabbage, folding itself, unfolds, or
as Mr. Thompson put it: nothing is faster than ice.

JOHN B. LEE

Falstaff as a Hockey Goalie: taking the Edge off

He stands in the black galaxies of the net
swishing left and right
where the whole pulsing universe
hums like a whip in the flesh of God.

And while scalding disks
bite his leather
in the mount and settle of their flacking hour
he wags like a lover's hammock —
his skates swabbing and weightless
as a hanged man's ticking feet.

But sometimes his nerves betray him
too fast, too slow, might
jitter a muscle like a fly-bit horse's rump.
So before the game he drinks
to get the edge off,
to slur his conducting arm
that rocks his open hand
or nurses the fever from his brow
or soothe his gut
calm him down to smoothness
the way a breakwall tames the sea
and thus he splays and shuts
and dives and clicks and flicks
within the tiny kingdom of his goal
where spine jerk's a bucking ram
and the thing that is the game
untwists with time
and flattens like a crumpled note
to read the noble madness of what's done
and drink a little more
until the print unsnarls
and the brain waves a sweet farewell
like a dreamy wife scented into the waning mystery.

The Hockey Player Sonnets

for Al Purdy

i
What about them Leafs, eh!
(expletive deleted*) couldn't score an (e.d.) goal
if they propped the (e.d.'s) up
in front of the (e.d.) net
and put the (e.d.) puck on their (e.d.) stick
and the (e.d.) goalie fell asleep
and somebody (e.d.) yelled, 'SHOOT THE (e.d.) THING!'
(E-E-E-E-D-eeeeeee.!!!!!!!)

ii
(e.d.)!!this (e.d.) shower's (e.d.) cold.
who the (e.d.) flushed the (e.d.) toilet?
give me the (e.d.) soap.
hand me that (e.d.) towel.
has anybody got some (e.d.) shampoo.
toss the (e.d.) over here!
thanks. what's this (e.d.) pansy (e.d.)?

who brought the (e.d.) beer?
toss me one. stop throwing that (e.d.) snow.
you could lose an (e.d.) eye.
and so on ...

iii
What do you mean you don't watch sports on TV.
Why the (e.d.) not?
Haven't you got an (e.d.) TV?
What the (e.d.) do you watch?
What the (e.d.) do you do?

Read!!! — who the (e.d.) wants to (e.d.) read!
too much like (e.d.) thinkin'.

there is much (e.d.) laughter at this.
and so it goes —
'what about them Leafs, eh ...'

*hereinafter referred to as 'e.d.'

Industrial League Hockey

Leaning against the factory wall
— victims of the night,
their smoky breath hanging like cut lamb's tails
in the air.
One rattles wax wrap open
to liberate a dry cheese sandwich
while others grumbled
by the engines groaning in the green-glass light behind
admiring the way the trucker
threads his long load backwards through the needle's eye
of a doorway
that sighs open exuding steam
like the slow and sexy exhalation of a movie star.
And it is men such as these
unjailed by their off hours
that come to play
and from the first angry moment
of their swarming
through the door onto the ice
I knew there would be trouble
from the burly cluster of their workworn knuckles
bristled with black hair.

One fellow wearing a helmet high
on a skull-bone brow
as thick as a cheap cafeteria dinner plate
came racing
his derailed motors
intent on some kind of mutilation
with all 12 seasons of eating concentrated
to sustain the monogrammed pig-iron slabs of his pectorals
smelted in the forge of a big-wombed dam
with a vigorous appetite
and forearms like a Spanish pirate.
These he hurled at liberal fancies
occasioned by a world-weary mind
to scribble
a confession concerning swans
in a river
and astonishingly alone in the inclination
to think of the grace
before the meat.

JOHN B. LEE

Sitting in the Grays with the Blues

Outside the Gardens before the Leaf's game
icicles clatter down
like hardware too heavy for a nail
the sky
is a vague and dissipating ghost
with snow falling softly
in whispered secrets
to the gutter fungussed with brown slush
by a sewer-grate kettle steaming in the street
where chestnuts roast over smuts
on a glass wagon
while comers and goers struggle against insignificance
puffing like knocked-together chalk brushes
their bodies wrapped against winter
like fragile postage
pass scalpers barking their commerce
making tawdry deals
in the petrol-stinking night.

Inside the gardens a man fingers his buttonhole
and climbs the Escher nightmare
past the R.E.M. of vertigo
where gravity loosens its grip
and he might slide down air.
From there he can watch the game
his eyes falconing the puck
while all around him
the fans are clucking fox-jawed
some dangerous with disappointment
some overwhelmed by coffee
brood about the exit rush
and the plot jump of weather going on without them,
meanwhile snow gathers to moss the parking lot
and ice knits its crooked scarves of traffic
where cold wields its authority over engines
that strangle awake under key clicks
and light blinks that probe the edgeless dark
and muss for an hour or two
beyond the groaning arches of the building
where kids stray-cat with crazy hair
and cigarettes thrown away lit
lie like whip marks on cement
and bums drink from bag ends
in a sick wrinkle by a doorway shelter.

Still later with the night-numbed clock
running like a dreaming dog
on the empty street
the first car away moves
tiny like the growing tip of a root
into the life source
of another city, another home.

The Trade that Shook the Hockey World

When Gretzky went to L.A.
my whole nation trembled
like hot water in a tea cup when a train goes by.

Something about Hollywood and hockey.
Something about Canadians in Babylon.
Something about gold and the gilded blades of grace.
Something about kings and the great republic.
Something about titans and the golden gods.
Something about the myth of boys and the truth of men.
Something about beer in the holy grail.
Something about the commodity of the human heart.
Something about the fast life …
fast food, fast cars, fast women, and a fastness.
But mostly something about moving too fast in time.

Taking Your Baby to the Junior Hockey Game

Watch for it to happen out there on the ice:
this music they fight for.
You can feel her beside you as though poised in front of a net
circling
circling.

Christ, you'll say,
baby if you were a forty-three-year-old Montreal potato merchant
I'd be your five-iron.
I would never dissolve, in the middle of a rush, passes coming snap snap
crossing the blue line barely on-side, never dissolve into adolescence fumbling
for control.
I would cleave
I would be your hawk
I would be silence.
Forests.
And baby, you'll say, if you conducted the Bach Society Choir in town
I'd be a dentist's wife
straining among sturdy contraltos after your unheard perfection
longing with them to devour your wrists, your boyish wit.
I would finish your every mad flight through the defence
with deft flicks to the lower-left and upper-right-hand corners,
inevitable, the momentary angel,
your right wing.

FLORENCE McNEIL

Hockey

The local players   close to the stars
unleash hydra arms across the shadows
their forms inflated
their artificial masks patterned with light
they are precise and intent
in their performance
The night has warmed
brown grass rumbles under their skates
another season prods them into more vitality
slush in their eyes
they smash at spring with fluid strokes
their minds do not bow to small foreshadowings
the inclusion of another victory
the electric claim of green things
silently   all ready
measuring the rink for its renewal

Meeting of the Animals

The oil executives have called
a meeting of the animals
interrupting the hockey game
to show us
Disney-eyed creatures
who look at each other with only
limited rancour
their decision to live
ratified by the company ecologists
their forests filtered through public relations
are like children's books
a sunlit ease in the twenty-four inch invasion
What we see are the coloured bonds
the two minute benevolence
the kindergarten bestiary
surfacing in perfect pastels
the Bambis whose gentle forms fade
into the second period
where intensive colours prefigure
a longer deception
and through the harsh reds and whites
figures
humped like buffalo
litter the plains of ice
with sticks as petrified and cold
as forgotten bones.

Guy Lafleur and Me

Guy Lafleur and me: both thirty-three,
both reaching those middle years.
And in yesterday's paper
extensive reports of Lafleur's announced retirement,
due to the fact that he's lost the edge mentally,
no longer has the confidence.
Though he now has the rest of his life
to look forward to — large salaries and endorsements —
for Guy the glory days are over,
his spirit crucified on the ice at the Forum,
the highpoints of his career
relegated to the trophy room.

Me I am just getting started,
just getting good. I am not losing speed.
I skate out onto the ice
at a crucial moment and easily put the puck
into the net. It is there, in the net. Look
at the stymied, perplexed goalie.

November 26, 1984

Ice Maker

when Ernie floods the rink
he lays five trout
with rhinestones in their eyes
on the grey cement
positions them at centre
turns the tap   flicks the switch
water spills   pushes fish forward
across the blue line

by night only rhinestones
glitter in the goal

Hockey Players

What they worry about most is injuries
broken arms and legs and
fractured skulls opening so doctors
can see such bloody beautiful things almost
not quite happening in the bone rooms
as they happen outside
And the referee?
He's right there on the ice
not out of sight among the roaring blue gods
of a game played for passionate stockbrokers
children wearing business suits
and a nation of television agnostics
who never agree with the referee and applaud
when he falls flat on his face

On a breakaway
the centreman carrying the puck
his wings trailing a little
on both sides why
I've seen the aching glory of a resurrection
in their eyes
if they score
but crucifixion's agony to lose
— the game?

We sit up there in the blues
bored and sleepy and suddenly three men
break down the ice in roaring feverish speed and
we stand up in our seats with such a rapid pouring
of delight exploding out of self to join them why
theirs and our orgasm is the rocket stipend
for skating thru the smoky end boards out
of sight and climbing up the appalachian highlands
and racing breast to breast across laurentian barrens
over hudson's diamond bay and down the treeless tundra where
auroras are tubercular and awesome and
stopping isn't feasible or possible or lawful
but we have to and we have to
laugh because we must and
stop to look at self and one another but
our opponent's never geography
or distance why
it's men
— just men?

And how do the players feel about it
this combination of ballet and murder?

For years a Canadian specific
to salve the anguish of inferiority
by being good at something the Americans aren't
And what's the essence of a game like this
which takes a ten year fragment of a man's life
replaced with love that lodges in his brain
                    and substitutes for reason?
Besides the fear of injuries
is it the difficulty of ever really overtaking
a hard black rubber disc?
— Boys playing a boy's game in a permanent childhood
with a screaming coach who insists on winning
sports-writer-critics and the crowd gone mad?
— And the worrying wives wanting you to quit and
your aching body stretched on the rubbing table
thinking of money in owners' pockets that might be yours
the butt-slapping camaraderie and the self indulgence
of allowing yourself to be a hero and knowing
everything ends in a pot-belly

Out on the ice can all these things be forgotten
in swift and skilled delight of speed?
— roaring out the end boards out the city
streets and high up where laconic winds
whisper litanies for a fevered hockey player
Or racing breast to breast and never stopping
over rooftops of the world and all together
sing the song of winning all together
sing the song of money all together

                    (and out in the suburbs
there's the six-year-old kid
whose reflexes were all wrong
who always fell down and hurt himself and cried
and never learned to skate
                    with his friends)

Homage To Ree-shard

Frog music in the night
and all the dogs and cats and cows
on farms for miles in all directions
screech and howl and moo from shore to shore
the beasts of God bust their guts with song
and the sun a great bonfire burning away
darkness on the lake's little republic
but so delicate a rose tint on water
no girl has steps as light
Hockey — we have been talking hockey

Dave Williams and me at Roblin Lake
then slept and I wake him up later
to witness this birth this death of darkness
but how it relates to hockey — don't ask
tho maybe frog-music frog-music
of Montreal and Ree-shard the Rocket
"First madman in hockey" Dave says
not sensible and disciplined
but mad mad mad I see him
with balls shining out of his eyes
bursting a straitjacket of six Anglos
riding his back a thousand miles
of ice to beat the Anglo goalie
while all the dogs and cats and cows
from Toronto to Montreal and Roblin Lake
and Plains of Abraham forever
moo and screech and howl from shore
to morning shore in wild applause

The first madman
first out-and-out mad shit disturber
after cosmic duels with Bill Ezinicki
now sullen castrated paranoid Achilles
with sore heel in a Montreal pub retired
to muse on wrongs and plot revenge
with long memories of broken storefronts
along St. Catherine Street
when Maisonneuve's city made him emperor
for a day and hour and a moment
But Dave if I may interject a comment
difficult tho that may be
I think compared to the Rocket
all Iron Horses Catfish Shoeless Joes
and the Bambino's picayune meal of a mere
planetary dozen steaks and hotdogs and mammoth
bellyache sink to a minor tribal folk tale

in a trivial game of rounders somewhere south
"Hockey" says Dave pontifically
"is the game we've made of all our myth
of origins a million snot-nosed kids
on borrowed bob-skates batting lumps
of coal in Sask and Ont and Que
between two Eaton's catalogues in 1910
these are the heroes these the Alexanders
of our foetal pantheon and you know
you eastern bastards froze in darkness
you don't know Bill Cook and brother Bun
they came from my town Lac Vert Sask
they came each spring showering ice cream
and chocolate bars on all the kids
in my home town they were the new gods
almost replacing money
and you could see they knew
they were the gods ..."

The sun now shines upon our right
out of the sea came he
for god's sake get ye hence to bed
no early risers we

And then I dreamed I dreamed Ree-shard
ancestor Maurice incestuous mythawful Rocket
standing at my bedside
I fled Him down the nights and down the days
I fled Him down the arches of the years
I fled Him down the labyrinthine ways
of my own mind — but he was too fast for me
his eyes blazing blowlamps
on Décarie and its cloacal hellway
and Montreal East kids with ragged *Canadien*
sweaters on St. Germain outside the factory
I worked in all the little Ree-shards
failing to negotiate contact
with their dream among the greasy-spoon
cafés and their out-of-work *peres*
and *meres* among the non-Anglos
among failed gangsters and busted drug peddlers
and '48 Pontiacs with bad lungs
coughing their own smoke in Montreal East
I dreamed Ree-shard and the kids
Me the failed athlete and failed lover
absurd idealist and successful cynic
I dreamed the bitter glory-fled old man

nursing his hate and grudges and memories
his balls making only sewer water
with Jung and Freud as solemn witnesses
But that man disappeared suddenly
and what took his place was the real thing
honest-injun Rocket indubitable Maurice
mad mad Ree-shard in fact the first and only
berserker astronaut among the lesser
groundlings their necessary flyboy
who slapped a star along Décarie hellway
and rang a bell in Bonaparte's tomb
and knocked a crumb from Antoinette's pastry
waved his wand at Anglos Howe and Ezinicki
and made Quebec Canadian

Rocket you'll never read this
but I wish for you all the best things
whatever those may be
grow fat drink beer live high off the hog
and may all your women be beautiful
as a black spot of light sailing among the planets
I wish it for just one reason
that watching you I know
all the things I knew I couldn't do
are unimportant

Night Star Special

This future Bobby Orr
bounds and rebounds off the boards,
his wooden stick a wielded sword,
his blades upon his feet.

This solitary night star chases
the swift hiss of his skatesong
on a rink racing powerplay speeding along.
Then! One sharp pass — the play's complete!

He fakes the invisible opposition.
Compressed pellet from his weapon shot —
An unchecked zoom that finds the slot!
He shoots! He scores! The goalie's down!

Everblue the nightsky light,
the crisp moon his only flood,
this hockey star with roaring blood
— avenging ghost of past defeats.

Skating with his late-night dreams
on a practice rink on the riverbank,
below the flowing toboggan track,
this phantom champion fleets.

Ice Time

cutting across a park in late November
I stop,
hear voices coming from the bottom
of an empty swimming pool.
a group of boys are playing hockey
with the yellow of a tennis ball.
I don't disturb them.
imagine, playing ball hockey
on the floor of an autumn pool.
the boys are warming up
taking shots from the shallow end
to the deep end.
goaltender finds it easier that way
and
he is using school bags for goalposts.
now that makes sense.
he is letting his friends learn
to put homework
where it should be,
in the middle
of an almost November dark.

Clearing

OK, let's go over clearing again

I'm telling you, boys
this game is so fuckin simple
anybody with half an ass an half a knee
could play it

now, when we get the puck in our end
it goes straight behind the net
to a defenceman

he puts it around the boards
to the open winger

now, the centre
who's bin watchin the slot
sees this an busts his arse up the middle
an the other winger
who's bin guardin his point
goes up with him

so, when the centre hits our blue line
that puck should be on his stick
an slicker'n shit off a shiny shovel
you got a two-on-one

now, alls we gotta do
is go through it a couple dozen times
an we got it

like I say, boys
this game is so fuckin simple

Once is Once Too Many

I only forgot to wear my can
once   that was enough

it was one time over in Glenavon
I went out for my first shift
and you know how when you're waitin
for the drop of the puck
you lean over and rest
your stick across your can
well, this time all I can feel
is wide-open spaces an the family jewels

but I'm not gonna skate
back to the bench
so I figger I'll get by
for this shift anyways

well, I'm all over the ice
like a mad man's shit and
I chase the puck into their corner
pass it back to Brian on defence
then head for the net to screen the goalie

when I look back at the point
sure as God's got sandals
Brian's just blasted one crotch-high

not to worry I figger
I'll just jump and let it cruise
between my legs

well, I couldnta timed'er
more perfect   it was just
like a three-ball combination

cept that two of them were
damn near in my throat
while the puck caroms into the net
like snot off a door knob

was I pleased?
is the Pope married?

The Way it Was

it's enough to give
a dog's arsehole the heartburn
you guys with your leagues
an drills an tactics
you're gonna kill this game
for the kids

when I started
the old lady just went into the porch
to our skate box
took the ones closest to my size
an laced them on
taped a coupla Eaton's catalogues
to my shins an sent me
over to the pond

all the kids were there after school
an from dusk to dark on weekends

the fat guys got to play net
the ones who couldn't skate so good
were on defence
an the best scorers were the forwards

an we only had one puck
so you either learned how to stickhandle
through twenty guys
or you never got to touch it

then some kids whose folks had no money
for skates would stand around
till one of us tuckered out
an they used ours

those were our practices
an if we got lucky
we'd play another town
maybe three, four times a year

an by the time you were eleven or so
the poor players were weeded out
an you were left with one team

that's how I learned

Hockey

winter time and the frozen river
sunday afternoon
they're playing hockey on the river
rosy ...
he'll have that scar on his chin forever someday his girlfriend will say
hey where ...
he might look out the window ... or not
you skate as fast as you can 'til you hit the snowbank
(that's how you stop)
and you get your sweater from the catalogue
you use your rubber boots for goal posts
ah ... walkin' home

don't let those sunday afternoons
get away get away get away get away
break away break away break away break away

this stick was signed by jean beliveau so don't fucking tell me where
to fucking go ...
oh sunday afternoon
someone's dog just took the puck — he buried it it's in the snowbank
... your turn
they rioted in the streets of montreal when they benched rocket
richard it's true

don't let those sunday afternoons
get away get away get away get away
break away break away break away break away

the sun is fading on the frozen river
the wind is dying down
someone else just got called for dinner
rosy
hmm ... sunday afternoon

Christmas-Morning Hockey

That one Christmas morning
when we'd opened all our presents
and the excitement had died,

we said, Let's go down
to Second Marsh and have
all the ice to ourselves,

but on our way there
stopped on Armadale Avenue
with our mouths opening wide,
then even wider,

as we saw Charlie Conacher
(looking very strange
out of Maple Leaf uniform)
standing out in the road,

shooting ten-foot-high pucks
at his pal Busher Jackson
one whole lamppost away
as the whole street looked on,

the Busher coming back
with shots almost as high,

and when we moved off
fifteen minutes later
they were still shooting rubber
on the ice-covered asphalt
as if they needed practice,

and we only hoped they'd save
a few of those hard ones
for the Bruins or the Red Wings
the next Saturday we tuned in
Hockey Night in Canada.

The Hockey Fan Hears the Muse

An answer is plain as the nose snuffling thick in his head. The radio broadcasts, the Hot Stove League, the two-minute interview, the post-game wrap-up, the leisurely between-period profile, dogs and all — or horses, sometimes there are horses — the yelling and hollering in rinks, in dressing rooms, in school playgrounds, the arguments in front of the common room, the family room, the beer parlour, television. The fan eats, sleeps and dreams stories. Consumes stories, gobbles them up, can't get enough. Reading lips on television you know inside stories, you know what the coach really said. Or in the pools you can play owner, pick your own team, curse and yatter at your bad picks, at players who don't perform, at the ungodly run of injuries.

Given to tell stories, he imagines a future and weaves into the present remembered and invented flashes of the past. In these stories he becomes part of a team again: reader and writer, playing.

Yes, in these stories you, dear reader, play at your own pace, hear the soft sounds of a tale unfolding, listen to the stroke of letters grazing the icy page. You make it go, make it go.

I see, she sings, I see you pass me, she sings, I see you past me. You pass me this book, she sings, skate on by, pass me the puck, pass me, pace me, she sings, paste me, taste me, how you gonna take me.

The Hockey Fan Reflects On Beginnings

It all begins with guts. The looping scrawl of prairie rivers tucked inside the cavity of your belly, chewing your food, as they say munch, munch. Just chomping and chewing and squirting and squeezing and squooshing mush diddle diddle mush, moving a lung, tickling the blood stream blood red, trickling along the vine of veins. Squish dee doodle go the guts. Squoik. Down the hatch, down the tube, the same old story: the teacher smears the ping pong ball with glycerine and squeezes it into the inner tube, bicycle tube, red with some blue blotches, tries to squeeze it down the tube, muscles working, grimace, grunt, stuck in the old tube, slammed shut, bunged up. Guts belong in your belly and you want to leave them there where they belong. Don't spill them however much you long to tell it all.

In Flin Flon he begins another beginning, a legendary place where the garden is called, yes, the Main Arena and the streets are paved with hockey pucks and gold. Or so the story goes and you never get away from the stories. Right now, on the desk in front of me, a May 1989 article in *The Hockey News* tells how the Swift Current Broncos come from the smallest town to win the Memorial Cup since the Flin Flon Bombers won in 1957. You see? You see?

Flin Flon? they say.

Why the only people I know from Flin Flon are hockey players and hookers.

My mother is from Flin Flon, you say.

Long pause.

And what position does she play?

Left Wing, Right Wing, Defence, Goal: the goal of life is.

Of course you expect stories from people raised in a town named after the nickname of a fictional hero. The hockey fan began in place and a good beginning it was. His mother worked hard to bear him. She carried him warm in her belly and then he was bare and she lugged him home in her arms. Her travail gave him from her to you, sitting there, lying there. A good beginning it was, but sometimes she can barely stand him.

Rules for a Hockey Story

1 For your starting line choose strong verbs up front with concrete nouns rock-solid on defence.

2 Use proper nouns — quick, quick, slide from one to another — throw the quick pass. Hockey is measured by the speed of the proper nouns, running and running. Pro nouns.

3 All common nouns and adjectives are to be preceded by obscenities which end in "ing."

4 Remember, nonetheless, that hockey is a sweet game and goalies are tender folk.

5 A hockey story is an anatomy. Catalogues, rosters, lineups, histories, biographies, statistics (home and away) are necessary. Include height and weight and scoring records and notes on position, disposition, indisposition. Tell of the time around scars, sprinkle liberally with clichés. There is no tomorrow, the tale has to move quickly. You have to give it all you got to take what you can get.

6 The narrative drives for the goal and the goal is a net framed by steel posts and struck into the ice, or milk tins or pieces of coal, or the corner of a garage and the garbage can — you know how it goes. The goal of life is. Yes, at the end of it all stands St. As Is, the big stopper. The end. Period.

7 The goal is the key, the goalie key, he keeps it going. The goalie wants the game to go on and on, he does not want you to draw first blood or any blood at all. The goalie is tender, the goalie is quick. He believes in delay. He wants you to try again.

8 Line changes make the game move smoothly. Watch out you don't get caught with too many men on the ice — all those proper nouns piled up in the corner. The ref'll getcha.

9 Shifts are desirable. The quick change of pace catches people up short.

10 You have a choice. You can skate around, throw a deke here, a deke there, a shift and wiggle, turn and hit a body. Bounce around like a soft puck or a bad cheque with no assets. Or you can have tactics. In prose the long line stretches like a poke check right across to the right hand margin, the boards, the tack catches you in the end. You turn a corner every time, like a tic, twitch when you approach the gutter or the edge of things. If you get a chance, slam. Slam him into the boards.

The Coach Reads the Signs

Our goalie has so many letters in his name you can find two alphabets. The letters ride up one side of his sweater, down the other and crisscross in the middle. Nobody knows for sure what his name is so we call him Al for short or Elf 'cause he's little too — dances a sprightly jig in the showers to escape the pontoon-foot guys, quick as a bunny.

But on the ice it's a different story. Al or Elf always slows things down. When he flops on the puck, he makes an alphabet soup and the refs start to read the story on his back and forget to blow the whistle. The other team digs out the puck to score before the refs wake up. It happens every game.

The coaches are going to send Al down. They say he takes too long to get up from the ice. Top-heavy they say. All those letters spell trouble.

Playing Time Is a Fiction

He thinks of playing time. I need playing time, he says, I need the time coach, I need the ice time. Playing. Ice time is the thing wherein I'll catch the fancy of the queen. Ice is the thing he says. I sing the puck.

On the other hand. Playing time does not equal real time. Play time is the gap between clock time and game time.

And then of course. Hockey turns on the number three, beginning, middle and end, delayed sometimes but an end nonetheless, often a modest closure, a tie, like kissing your sister. If you go into overtime you have sudden death or sudden victory. Either way there's no tomorrow, they say. And what's wrong with kissing your sister?

But still. Clock time is ten seconds of silence before the beginning of the long dash.

Even though. At this very moment an island floats slowly across the Canadian Arctic. Within twenty years it will be in the United States and then later in the Soviet Union, floating all the time.

Scouting Report: Floats around centre ice. Leaves a big gap between himself and the dee. Spreads his legs like that and sooner or later he'll get a kick between the big toes with a frozen snowshoe.

Nevertheless. Playing time is a fiction. He likes to play, play it out, string it out more and more. Until a period gets in the way, breaking time though he tries to play right through, and in the end he wheezes after each shift. Gobs of phlegm rattle in his throat. His ass droops and his belly sags but he keeps going. Tells himself he can go again but time catches up anyway. We all get it in the end. One scything sweep check stops you cold or the big butt end knocks you tits up, suckers skyward and they put you on ice.

But as I said before. In the middle fiction is play time and outside the rink, off ice, the universe winds down or winds up, stretches and delivers. Ozone breaks down or builds up. Great streams of gases shoot off our galaxy, they say, people molest each other in the usual ways, the Middle East is middling quiet for the Middle East, bibliothumpers browbeat and harangue, bully bash and murder in the name of right, people everywhere duck the dentist, pay the piper, shake the social worker, badger the butcher, kick the cat. The sun groans after last night's shaker and comes with a great noisy crack. A head-splitting dawn spilling too bright words spells HANGOVER in Braille on the wet side of your eyelids. Still, bellybuttons collect lint, stains colour your lover's underwear, glass shatters in the street, socks get lost in the dryer. And, in spite of the strides of regimentation and definition, the galaxy hurtles along, a stitch in time, while love is no more gentle than it should be and scotch whiskey, my love, amber warm in the goblet, makes its way overseas for the betterment of humankind and the ease of mid-life crises, both yours and mine.

Neat is it. Take it neat? Want some ice?

He said.

Moreover.

Hockey Haiku

Men are like
the Toronto
Maple Leafs:

they lose,
they keep
selling out.

Fifty Mission Cap

Bill Barilko disappeared
that summer
He was on a fishing trip
The last goal he ever scored
won the Leafs the cup
They didn't win another
'til 1962
the year he was discovered
I stole this from a hockey card
I keep tucked up under

My Fifty Mission Cap
I worked it in
to look like that

Bill Barilko disappeared
that summer (in 1950)
He was on a fishing trip (in a plane)
The last goal he ever scored (in overtime)
won the Leafs the cup
They didn't win another
'til 1962
The year he was discovered

My Fifty Mission Cap
I worked it in
to look like that

December River Blues

Winter comes
again the river sings
of shinny
sounds in frozen coves
young boys
skate ritual patterns
Inland (at night's edge)
the stands fill
slowly, with weekend devotees
but it's not the same

now there are too many teams and players
names to remember
lesser lights have become
stars with heavy blades
old warriors witness
their own demise
like faded hockey cards
hidden in countless bunks
lost in forgotten
attics of seasons past

winter comes again
the bones of old streetcars
rust in cold slow silence
modern buses on steel belted radials
deposit fans, rooters and supporters
(same thing)
at the doors of shinny shrines
to observe
le grand ballet sur glace
seasoned eyes note
the mounting score
of fashion designer uniforms
depositing youths' harvest
in strained harmony
of contract and desire

old heros sit at neon interviews in
between
periods and wear their scars
like old numbers

while they answer questions (for the record)
about their passion
                    holding the memory of what
was

winter returns
                still the skaters come

BASEBALL

If there really is a heaven baseball
certainly must be played there …
— Al Purdy

Baseball, a poem in the magic number 9

for Jack Spicer

1

The white sphere
turns, rolls
in dark space

the far side of one destroyed galaxy,
a curve ball
bending thru its long arc
past every planet of our dream.

A holy spectre of a curve ball,
dazzling white, brand new
trademark still fresh:
"This is a regulation Heavenly League Baseball"

O mystic orb of horseshoe stitching!
Hurled from what mound in what Elysian field,
    from what mound, what
    mystical mount,
                where what life-bringing stream?

God is the Commissioner of Baseball.
Apollo is the president of the Heavenly League.
The Nine Muses, his sisters
        the first all-girls baseball team.
Archangel Michael the head umpire.
Satan was thrown out of the game
        for arguing with the officials.

In the beginning was the word, & the word was
"Play Ball!"

Now that white sphere
cools,
& the continents
rise from the seas.

There is life
on Baseball.

The new season is beginning.
Zeus winds up to throw out
the first ball
like a thunderbolt.

Take me out
                    to the ball
                                    game.

2

July in Oliver, cactus drying
in the vacant lots,

in the ball park, the Kamloops Elks
here for a double header, Sunday

baseball day in Oliver, day of worship
for me.

          At the park an hour early,
scribbler full of batting averages,

sometimes I got a steel basket
& sold hotdogs, peanuts, sometimes

I pickt up a broken bat, lugged it home
& taped it, not so much for batting

as for my collection. Louisville Slugger.
My father was official scorer,

high in the chicken wire box
on top of the grandstand, he was tough

on the hitters, as later I was,
pens & pencils in front of me. Oliver

nearly always won, the cars parkt
around the outfield fence honking

for a hometown rally, me quieter,
figuring out the percentage, a third the age

of the players, calculating chances
of the hit & run play.

                              Later,
I was official scorer, they knew

I had the thick rule book memorized.
Sweat all over my face, eyes squinting

thru the chicken wire, preparing
batting averages & story for

the Oliver *Chronicle*.

3

Manuel Louie, old Manuel Louie
is chief of the Indians around Oliver.
1965 now, he is 94, but looks 55.
He's still got big black mustache, shoots pool
with his belly hanging over the rail.

Age 80, he was still playing Indian baseball games,
the chief, bowlegged running bases with turkey feather
in his hat.

The Wenatchee Chiefs, class A,
were spring training in Oliver then,
letting Manuel Louie work out at shortstop, weird Sitting Bull
  Honus Wagner,
in exchange for his steam bath, that's how he lookt 40
at age 80, a creek beside his house, mud hut full of steam.

That year the Wenatchee Chiefs finisht fifth.

4

The New York Yankees
are dying this year, the famous pinstripe uniform
covered with dust of other ballparks.

Mickey Mantle is a tired man with sore legs,
working at a job. Roger Maris forgotten
on the sports pages, a momentary spark
turned to wet ash.

A beanball on the side of the skull
killed a ballplayer
when I was a kid,
it was violence
hidden behind the grace of base-
ball.

Now Warren Spahn is trying
to win a few more games
with his arm 44 years old,
in the National League
where no pitcher's mound
is Olympus.

& Willie Mays is after all
sinew & flesh
as a baseball
is string & leather,

& when baseballs get old
kids throw them around,
torn horsehide flapping
from that dark sphere.

> I was in love with Ted Williams.
> His long legs, that grace,
> his narrow baseball bat
> level-swung, his knowledge of art,
> it has to be perfect, as near
> as possible, dont swing
> at a pitch seven centimeters
> wide of the plate.

I root for the Boston Red Sox.
Who are in ninth place.
Who havent won since 1946.

It has to be perfect.

5

In the nineteenth century
baseball came to the Pacific Northwest.

Mustache big muscled ballplayers of beer barrels
among bull lumberjacks & puffsteam train engines,
mighty trees of rainforest, pinstripe uniforms,
those little gloves of hurt hand, heavy bats of yore,
baseball in Seattles & Vancouvers of the past when Victoria
was queen of Canada, Manifest Destiny of the ballpark
cut into swathe of rainy fir trees.

Now still there — I go to see the Vancouver Mounties
of minor league green fence baseball playing
Hawaii of the Pacific, Arkansas Travelers of gray visitors garb,
I sit in warm sun bleachers behind first base
with Keep-a-movin Dan McLeod, bleach head poet of the Coast
gobbling crack shell peanuts — he's sitting beside me,
gadget bag full of binoculars & transistor radio, tape recorder,
cheering for the Mounties, nuts, they are Dominicans of the North,
dusky smiling on the lucky number souvenir program,
where I no longer write mystic scorekeeper numbers in the little squares,
sophisticate of baseball now, I've seen later famous players here.

What are you doing, they ask,
young esthete poet
going to baseball games,
where's your hip pocket
Rimbaud?

I see the perfect double play, second baseman in the air legs tuckt
over feet of spikes in the dust, arm whipping baseball
on straight line to first baseman, plock of ball,
side's retired, the pitcher walks head down quiet from the
mound.

6

The herring-
bone stitching
takes one last
turn
till Louisville Slugger
cracks
& the spin
changes, a cleat
turns in the
sod, digs earth,
brown showing
under green,
bent knee takes
pressure.

Lungs fill
with air,
pump-
action legs, foot

pounds on narrow
corner of the bag, rounding
                                        the body leans
                                        inward, eyes
                                        flick up once
                                        under cap, head
                                        down, legs running,
                                        buckle!

& the fire that breaks from thee then told a million
times
              since 1903,
              the first
              World Series, white sphere
              turns, the world again
              spun around once, the sun
              in October again sinking
              over the pavilion roof
              in left field.

This story is for you, Jack, who had eyes to see
a small signal
from the box
                            more than 90 feet
                            away.

7

When I was 12 years old I had a baseball league
made of a pair of dice, old home-made scorebooks,
National Leagues, American Leagues, Most Valuable Players!

The St. Louis Browns played the Chicago Cubs in the World Series!
The Yankees finisht in seventh place, the batting championship
went at .394. It was chance, roll of dice, blood doesnt tell
in that kid's bedroom season —

                                                                        I was afraid to try out
                                                                        for the Oliver junior league team,
                                                                        I would strike out
                                                                        every time

                                                                        till I was sixteen,
                                                                        oldest you could be, & played
                                                                        one game before my summer job,

& I hit a bases loaded single
in the first inning. I was the
tallest kid on the team.

But I bought Sport magazine & Baseball Digest, & knew all
the numbers. Ty Cobb's lifetime batting average was .367, I remember now,
Rogers Hornsby's lifetime batting average was .354. In 1921 Babe Ruth hit
59 home runs.

Ty Cobb was better than Babe Ruth.
Ted Williams was better than Joe DiMaggio.
I like the Boston Red Sox who are in ninth place.

I still play that game, I think.
I'm sitting at my desk in my bedroom right now.

8

Nine.
Is a baseball number.
Nine innings.
Nine players.
Ted Williams was the best hitter of all time,
& the number on his back was nine.

Here is today's lineup:

1f	Terpsichore
2b	Polyhymnia
rf	Clio
lb	Erato
3b	Urania
cf	Euterpe
ss	Thalia
c	Melpomene
p	Calliope

A lineup like that is enough to inspire
the faithfulness of any fans of the good art
of baseball.

I have seen it happen
to the best poets
of this summer
& last.

9

Long shadows
fall across the infield
in the ninth inning.
Sometimes ball players
look like they're dying
as they walk off the field
in the dusk.

I knew an old man in San Francisco
came to life
when the Dodgers were in town.
Now he is dead, too,
& Jack is dead,

& the soldiers play baseball
in Asia,
where there is no season,
no season's end.

"It's just a game,"
I used to be told,
"It isn't whether you win or lose,
but how you
play the game."
In baseball
that is how you say
the meek shall inherit
the earth.

September 30, 1965,
Willie Mays has 51 home runs,
gray hair
at his temples,
he says he has been
getting tired
for six years.

I know I feel my own body
wearing down,
my eyes watch
that white ball
coming to life.
Abner Doubleday
lived in the nineteenth century,
he is dead,

but next spring
the swing of a
35 ounce bat
is going to flash with sunlight,
& I will be a year
older.

My nose was broken twice
by baseballs.
My body depends on the game.
My eyes
see it now on television.
No chicken wire —
it is the aging process.
The season
can't help but measure.

I want to say only
that it is not a
diversion of the intelligence,
a man breathes differently
after rounding the bag,
history, is there such a thing,
does not
choose, it waits & watches,
the game
isnt over till the last man's
out.

September 1965

Parc Jarry 1969

There are thirty thousand aluminum
seats at Jarry Park, and on Bat Day
fifteen thousand kids are banging
free miniature Louisville Sluggers on them.

A not quite major league noise, but
if you enjoy clang and can tolerate
a guy playing a violin on the Expos' dugout roof
you'll put up with it.

To be almost major league,
to watch Bob Gibson walk in
from the dressing room at the right field foul pole.

There's no grandstand, just metal bleachers all around,
and a guy in a toque
who buys a seat beside him behind third
for his duck, a leash on its neck.

Even in the out of town papers
there's Montreal listed in the National League standings,
and my New Yorkish Cornell Berkeley buddy Ed Pechter
eats five hotdogs, no mustard, no relish.

But jeepers, Jarry Park. They play softball
just outside left field, kids kick their feet
in the pool just past right. This is
a community park, what's Cincinnati doing here?

Olympic Stadium 1977

Dwight Gardiner led me out of the Metro,
across some concrete and through a door

into a loud burst of light, huge circle
of yellow, red, blue, and special green!

Still batting practice, I saw a bat flash
and then crack, crack, crack, cra-hack

echoed round the abandoned legend, a ghost
of the games. We settled in. Four attendants

sold us beer. I saw eight people in uniforms
dusting off seats in one empty section.

This is labour in Quebec. Eventually
somebody came to bat, probably San Diego,

my kind of luck. Yes, I said to Dwight, he's
back this week from Bolivia, it is *très grand*

but everything is so far away — the infield,
the National League pennant, America.

High above, the disc of grey-blue sky
is empty. At least at little Parc Jarry

we could watch the new Boeing 747s
hang in the low sky. If the score was

St. Louis 10, Expos 0, we could
look over the right field fence, check out

the swimmers in the pool, the kite fliers
with their daddies Sunday afternoon.

Exhibition Stadium 1986

Going to the game with David McFadden
you really need three seats,
such as here above the flat fog,
last game of the season, KC in town.

He has a thick jacket and a big shoulder bag.
We climb steep stairs to the top,
huge hoagies in our hands, I cant escape
the alliteration, that's how to fix this,
and really big waxy cups of Pepsi or something.

He settles like a hen on a dozen eggs,
puts down Pepsi and one-bite-gone hoagie;
out comes portable radio with ear plugs (good citizen),
out comes home-made scorebook, printed on computer.

Out come field glasses to catch signs
off runner at second getting them off catcher,
who gets them with turn of head out of dugout;
out comes Toronto Maple Leafs baseball cap.

Out comes Captain Midnight decoder fountain pen,
out comes one-dollar cigar, out comes Blue Jay yearbook,
McFadden takes a bite out of hoagie,
out comes sauerkraut all over fan in second-last row.

All right, the fog clears for a while, gulls descend,
Jesse Barfield hits home run number forty
and strikes out every other appearance. Every time
Lloyd Moseby comes up I yell
"Come on, Quaker!" McFadden says "Shaker!"

Then Dave lifts the plug out of one ear.
"He's hitting .271," he says. I remember
this is the lad who started a poetry magazine
in Hamilton, Ontario, imagine that!

Nat Bailey Stadium 1987

Sitting in famous Section 9 with our friends,
we see a wide purple sunset,
silhouette hillside with besom cedar trees,
a first place team gettin by on pitching.

Triple A uniforms can be a little embarrassing,
word too long on the hat, too much yellow and red on the visitors;
there are only three umpires, sometimes two,
the organist doesnt know his job, plays older goldies.

"The prettiest park in professional baseball."
"The most beautiful city in the world."
Some idiots in Section 8 bring their cellular phones.
Yes, we're more world-class than world-class Toronto.

But come on, you're with Fast Eddie & Paulie,
it's the sixth inning, a little dew in the night air —
where would you rather be? Some cathedral in Seville?
You want them to move the Canadians and the Phoenix Firebirds
under the dome downtown?

Never win a year's supply of Pepsi-Cola,
never attend when the Famous Chicken is in town,
sit down resolutely when some drunk boys try to start a wave,
applaud the number eight batter who hits a grounder behind the runner.

And when you go home, if you have to go home,
maybe there will be highlights on the TV news.

Oliver Community Park 1948

Familiar sun
declined is hasting now with prone career
to the Ocean Isles, and rising are some few bedraggled stars,

not to mention what I recall of my home town
ball field, 1990, weather-grey wooden grandstand
that would crash like a giant accordion
if four strong infielders full of beer
lined up and gave it a good shove.

We took oranges to the ball field, later
used the skins to cup water from the tap.

Willy and I wandered the perimeter trying to sell
Orange Crush and peanuts in the shell.
Other Sundays we pursued foul balls
through the deep rattlesnake grass for Elks Club dimes.

Once, age fifteen, I hit a single
with the bases loaded, but went next week
for work out of town,
where I still am,
and that was my real career.

They don't play ball there now, television
and the golf courses arrived,
highways became easy to use, money dropped by.

The tall wooden grandstand with the roof
stood through four decades of winters,
forty years of family picnics elsewhere,
power boats on small green lakes.

I went to
Quebec, I forgot the P.A. announcer's voice echoing
off the center-field scoreboard.

Ted Williams

Ted Williams never wearing a tie,
holding a bat in his hands in the dugout,
figuring the percentages,
enjoying bone-fishing
to be the best.

                    But flying a fighter plane
in two wars. Ted Williams, officer.

Angela waits
        for me to learn
about my heroes, learn
        to love life.

She is right.

Muhammed Ali is my hero,
he is the best,
he wont fight in the war now.

But
Ted Williams spit at the crowd
of collective buyers.
        He's maybe
second best.

May, 1967

Fielding

for my father

"Thanks for eveything" you quietly tell us
boldly for you who never knew quite how to
say such things with any ease
as we load our girls and luggage
into the car heading once more back to Winnipeg
and you pack your coffee and science fiction
into the cardboard box that is to see you
through the day watching alone
over a monstrous claw that
needs only the iron bones to rise
rigid behind it to rip off the overburden
sandy earth in abandoned fields
sealing the darkness sown 40 feet beneath us

where driven by thistles and dust
you spent your prime
stood knee deep in water
steeping in those strange long holes
punched coal from layers of packed clay
picking fire out of gleaming black seams

no place for any man
certainly no place for a young man like you
tempered to life by a thin white disc
that scraped inside your lungs   gently
with its sharp metal breathing

that was no place for you to be   father
far below the wasted prairie slamming its way
above you / above you
the baseball diamonds you told me about
where Clarey Weir ran 5 miles
from his father's dairy farm every game
to catch pop-ups in his hip pocket
and Barney Krivel swung under liners
in centre field with his back to the plate
and where you yourself pasted baseballs
through the Thirties / your twenties
using that ridiculous stubby glove I found
in the attic on the farm one day

you a sunburned farmer born to the prairies
held hard to the place
holding in the peak of your firm strength
those smooth wooden bats and angular picks

like they all did   all the men who stayed on
stood swinging at the round blurs
firing white past them
knelt digging in lignite
crumbling pockets of brown carbon

I remember you
years later in the white light
bent on our '55 Massey
dragging the rusted discer
over Evendon's section 7 miles north of town
its steel plates glinting on the rub of dirt
and the loud sudden scrape of rocks
grinding off sparks
your striped engineer's cap ruling the redness
in a clean line across your forehead

(the startling white softness of your body
underneath the gray cotton shirt you always wore)
and the sweet smell of the soap and cream
you pulled through the zipper of
your pebble-grained leather shaving kit
on Saturday nights and how in good spirits
we rolled down the gravel road
over the big hill under
the orange slant of the sun
with Hank Snow blowing us down into Estevan
from CHAB in Moose Jaw yellow
on the radio of our '53 green Ford
    Just to think it could be
    Time has opened the door
    And at last I am free
    I don't hurt anymore
and how the new mercury vapour street lights
would take us in their blueness past
the dazzling forkclinks and the lemonhalibut smells
fanning from the Canada Cafe
direct to the onoffonoffon incandescence drawing us
dreaming into the deep violet shade of the Orpheum theatre
where for 15 cents we witnessed
Gene Autry "the singing cowboy"
rescuing forlorn women in flickering melodrama

now the sunburn has almost gone from your neck
and the blackness is receding from your hair
but your hardened wrists
still thicken and move
after all these years
as we shake hands
and we see again
the light that has always sat / sits now
in the brown of your eyes
the slight halt that rests in your words

Bases

Father towered over
me, a silhouette,
a crack of bat and ball.

Remember Saturdays,
the home-plate maple
tree, a rosebud blooming
in a catcher's glove.

"Run like me," he'd say "with
dignity." Base to base
pockets full of bumblebees.

A lifted arm,
a victory, a maple
tree boosted to the sun.

A world of weekdays
now, father walks, a bunted
ball clumsy in the grass.

"See," he says, "the maple
tree has grown so tall
it pokes right through the sky."

These days I tower
over father, a glaring
memory, more solid
than a silhouette.

Savouring it all
we lean together
on the maple tree — bats
propped up against a wall.

The Baseball Hall of Fame

She had always wanted to play baseball, eight letters, an octave
of motion. So when she started driving taxi for a living
she tuned the radio to the ballgame and turned the car down
Toronto streets. Toronto grew up, grew old, grew older.
Old enough to move up to the majors. Not keys, but leagues.
Minor leaves fluttered through webs of memory in oldtimer's
mouths. *Sunnyside. Hanlan's Point. Babe Ruth.* She knew
the stories. The volume. Statistics erupted.

She always wanted to play baseball so when she drove
the taxi she said she wouldn't unless it turned out it
had a radio, AM, she said. That's the kind of girl I am.
Ain't touching no car without a radio.
And she didn't.

And when she went to the park and when it rained. Sun would shine
but she would find a pocket of rain and zip it up. Stands
smelling of memories. Jackson and Cobb and Chapman and
FitzGerald and *tell Carl it's okay.* She just wants to play.

The mound. Eyes following the line to the mound and Venus,
she thought Venus, invariably, and wanting, always wanting to
play, she thought inches, feet. Ninety feet. Nightly rituals.
Daily desires. She undressed to the national anthem. Waning.
She couldn't see the lights.

She never made the majors. She wound up and let a slow
curve continue until it covered the field, the line,
the composition. She always wanted to play baseball
but baseball had a heart of its own. She stuffed the mitt
in the backseat window and picked up low stations
and milked the meter and went to the games.

She wanted to play baseball and when the Blue Jays came
to town she painted it red. Some sense to the chaos of driving.
Slick city now: Car wielding fenders and carburetors and pistons
and alternators. A lot of horsepower. Slant six. Ball four. Fury.
Took a lot to warm it up but she cruised by hitters and they never
came close to her change-up. Her over. Her out.

She wanted to play. Spent years gently creasing pages
of southpaw dreams, scratches of sweet sliding heavenly bodies.
Everything forgotten. The time, place, space. A question
of physics. She had the positions down. Watched the 1-6-4
and knew.

She carried bits of mythology in worn pockets and scribbled new stats
she studied under moon. Stitched craters. Hovering over the plate.
That kindness of protection.

But she wanted, needed, desired and eventually she did. Became
the game and each team the moment she played hard. Hard ball.
Hard hitter. Straight shooter. And clichés grew around her night
vision, mare, her *sea of heartbreak*, her moon over heartache.

She mounted a sea of taxi and let loose. Curved down thruways
and lanes and crescents and highways and ain't it a bitch? Late, late
and street-empty she rode the crest of the Avenue Road hill watching
taxis float ghostly down to Davenport, swans, similes carved in wheels.

She had Clancy and she had Fernandez and she had McLain and she had
sweet bugger all. That's what happened. That's what hit her. She jumped.
Drove off to the northwest and set up shop in marriage. Said yes, I do,
I do too. Picked up a sucker and made him her own. Guy never knew the score.

So she always and after she packed in the taxi and retired
the glove and took her a husband, she found some sort of uneasy
alliance, some little-league consolation in cooking tired bacon and eggs
and remembering *easy over, strike three, you're out.*

And forgetting the grand slam.

How Do You Spell Relief?

for Hugh Hood

Midnight and the clips manage a manic arrangement
on the screen; somewhere the reenactment of the seventh
inning occurs and occurs and winces in full colour;
the reminder, the replay, the lack of.

And, how to you *spell* relief? Bring in the terminator
from another channel/league, a different wavelength? Bring in the ace
stopper (in the hole), watch the left hand's precision unfold slo-
mo terrific? Imagine Willie rising on the right side of a star?

Concentrate. Each wild pitch out of your control as the kite
red sun sets infinitely blue in the moonlight window, hangs
disconsolate while eyes gnaw the heart of a dilemma —
to go beyond and get out of the inning, this game.

Think over plays in fields memorized without originals backing
accurate imagining; the way only Roger Angell can call a season dulcet;
the way George Bowering can call a muscle move, a pitch, a game before
the action knows its inspiration, cause, effect.

Relief. Heart-hazed soft sun/moon evenings; the stands forgotten
as the bases fill up and grand slams glaze intaglio the superimposed
fields. The go-ahead in the batter's box and here comes the pitch
and it's a swing and a miss. And it doesn't matter. And it does.

Line Drives

Heart held in the glove of abeyance, suspended animation, so much
the space of need in the shape of love. Little things. *Do wah diddy.*
The way your smile breaks the barrier reef of this porcelain madness.
The ubiquitous hit parade, made less magical than necessary, more romantic
than possible. *Met him on a Monday and my heart stood still.* Till Friday.
Moon comes down to kiss water, throws a life line of heart to save this
drowning image.
Need of another, desire of desire, the end of innocence signals the thread
of regret,
weaves the night eccentric. Slides romance between the leaves of love.

Baseball, I desert you against my best intentions, deny your stunning
order, lack of chaos, prayer of perfection. Such beauty I cannot bear.

LEONARD GASPARINI

Junk Ball

When the last batter struck out
Dozens of autograph hounds
Ran in pursuit of their quarry
Who had just pitched a no-hitter.
One of them, an old junkie
Whose pockmarked face was familiar,
Moved in for the kill.
He carried no autograph book but himself.
Removing his sunglasses,
He accosted the knuckleball pitcher:
"Son, with an arm like yours
I could have a picnic!"

The Tease of Tiger Town

Maggie T eases a rented Lada
thru Customs
crossing the border
into Detroit —
she's heard of Lindell's bar
aches to snuggle up with
Dave Rozema
to squeeze the
Tiger relief pitcher's arm,
smell his thick
dark hair
Who says I like rock stars only?
& Maggie T also wants to cubbyhole
herself in the Tiger clubhouse
to breathe in
sweaty athletic
bodies
Better than any old politician
jogging up & down padded aisles
of a silver jet
that streaks thru
forests &
unemployment
Nothing like a ball player
to make me grovel
Let me sit with my Stroh's
& a hot dog & I'll wink
at Dave or maybe
trail big Jack Morris
into the bullpen
& chase love
into the
strike zone
& if things get boring
Maggie T will walk on water
take a stroll over the Detroit River
curtseying to sail boats
shouting back at
Greek sailors leering
from steamers at
her high-cut bathing suit
She calls this her public life
& from there
the Canadian border seems flat & boring
A Holiday Inn winces
in embarrassment at
her antics

on the polluted
water at
night
She ought to have stayed
at the ball park
People stand & stare at me
They're not looking at what I can do
They're not watching me fly
They're gawking at my body
But Maggie T spits back —
Well I've got nothin' on
honey so come
& stare at
Maggie Tease
'cause that's
who I am
Hang on to
my flight as I sail
over the river
a dove drifting
against wind
just before
a storm
I am turning heads
but I am touching minds
I am Beauty
I am Grace
I am Mystery
& I ought to be
available

Running (and Ground)

In the summertime
dusk came late
to the village
and our playground

Settled like ash
on our eyes
on the arc our
arms made swinging
(made the white ball
wobble, blurred
and oblong)

Settled like silt
on our eyes
on the grass
(mysteriously wet)
blurred the paths
our feet had grooved
between first and
second, third and
home

Ash from the last
cinder of sun
over First Bush

Silt from the
endless burning and
burning out of the
smoky volcanic light
the sky gave
to our names
and took back
with him into the
Indian-giving darkness.

Eyes bruised
by this strange dust
we gave up the
oblong ball, the
casual grooves —

sought those
other paths the
ground had saved
for us and this
occasion

As night came
down upon our games
we felt the
earth quake
at the cindrous rim,
the great Lake rolled
in her bed
with a trembling
of cleft water ...

and running now:
feel of body's
bounce on the
black blowing
out of whatever hole
the sky had left,

my heartbeat
swam before me
(in midnight lakes
bulb-eyed fish
thrash with nightmares
dream of
        quick sun
        sprouting mud
        greenish legs
        grass and
                running)

And running now
into or out of
remembering what
place this was
and running now
away from and toward
looking for bases
or home
and running now
till either my
body or I
caught up with the
ground, found
again the grooves
of other paths

more ancient feet
had stamped in the
first mud

(before the beaches dried)
those other paths
that caught our
stride in a
green running and
drew a distance
round our village
so first or second
try, or third
we rounded
perfect bases,

And running
            oblong
            crooked
            swinging
we ended all
our games
with home.

Four Questions for George Bowering

Michelin Green Guide: "The University [of Bologna], founded in 11C, had 10,000 students in 13C. At that time the professors were often women and a solemn chronicler reports that one of them, Novella d'Andrea, was so beautiful in face and body that she had to give her lectures from behind a curtain to avoid distracting pupils."

You who wrote Kerrisdale Elegies,
tell me:

Does the body teach us nothing?
What is it that we seek to learn
instead of beauty?
What do they mean, "distracting her pupils"?

I too once lectured in Bologna.
It was February, the room was cold,
I was more than adequately dressed.
No one put up a curtain.

What would happen if, just as you
slid into home plate,
the pitcher threw the catcher
an orange?

Softball:

grows along the fringe of industry and corn.
You come upon it out of thick
summer darkness, floodlights
focussing a neighbourhood or township: way to
fire, way to mix, way to hum.
Everything trim,
unlike life: Frost Fence, straight
basepaths of lime, warm-up jackets worn by
wives and girl friends in the bleachers
match the uniforms performing on the field.

Half-tons stare blindly from the sidelines.
Overhead
unnoticed nighthawks flash past the floodlights effortlessly
catching flies: way to
dip, pick, snag that sucker,
way to be.

Down here everyone is casual and tense,
tethered to a base.
Each has a motive, none
an alibi.
The body is about to be discovered.

He peers in for the sign, perfect order
a diamond in the pitcher's mind.
Chance will be fate, all
will be out.   Someone
will be called to arabesque or glide
                                        someone
muscular and shy

will become the momentary genius of the infield.

The Agony of Being an Expos Fan

It's like having your finest innocent hopes shattered, your heart ground to dust. Your pancreas has been removed and now you must eat pure sugar.

You have many questions that will always remain unanswered. What was the cosmic attraction between Ron Leflore, Tim Raines, Terry Francona and the left field wall? Who stole Steve Rogers' fastball? Was Rodney Scott the finger in the dyke? Did Bill Lee put a macrobiotic curse on the team? Was John McHale in league with the devil? Whatever happened to the team of the eighties (you suspect it was traded or sold down the river)?

You watched the current team play, and sigh. You miss Al Oliver, Gary Carter, Scott Sanderson, the Spaceman; you miss what never will be. In your worst nightmares Rick Monday's homer just clears the fence. You wish they would sell the team, or put it out of its misery.

It's like watching John Keats *not* die, and then he goes on to become a second-rate hack somehow.

Baseball

When I was a kid growing up in New York City I used to root for the Yankees. The Yankees always won, or so it seemed to me at age ten.

When I became a teenager I dropped the Yankees and started rooting for the Mets. In their first season, I even went to a game at the Polo Grounds, before they tore it down. Everybody knew the National was the tougher league. Rooting for the Mets was exquisitely painful, just like adolescence. When I was eighteen they won it all: the pennant, the Series, everything. The night they clinched the pennant from Atlanta I had my first meaningful sexual encounter.

When I was a young poet in my twenties, publishing my first books and wanting to be famous, I rooted for the Expos. That was after a number of years of rooting for nobody at all. The Expos never failed to disappoint, always failing, in the final analysis, to clinch anything. And of course I never became famous.

Now I am almost forty. I live in New England and root for the Red Sox. The Sox have always been a team with character; it's a character that comes from never garnering the ultimate prize. They play dramatic baseball, but they never win the big games. They haven't won the series since 1918. And they lose in ways you can never anticipate.

The Failure of Baseball

The failure of baseball
to uplift my heart this spring
is a curious thing.

I have no patience
for the disabled pitcher,
the slumping third baseman,

the team that can't get motivated.
I want every game
to be perfect, played

beneath a cloudless sky.
The mortals
who inhabit the game these days

are poor replacements
for the baseball gods
of my faultless youth.

The Hawk

The man is the consummate ballplayer:
he can hit, throw run, flag down
the most wicked line drives to center field,
steal a base when it's necessary
or just desired, gun down runners
at the plate, and, batting, make the ball fly
as if it had wings.

And though, this season,
his knees are shot
and he's been relegated to right field,
though he's struggling at the plate
and in the heat of July hitting around .230,
making errors and slowing down

just look at him playing
between these lines:
Andre Dawson, at the height of career,
Within this poem
he's at the top of his game
forever.

KEN NORRIS

Ode to Baseball

All summer
I'll sit in your bleachers, Baseball,
watching the game, catching some sun.
In an unintellectual season
it is a joy to witness gracefulness,
the pivoting shortstop,
an impossible catch
made up against the centrefield fence.
What the mind turns over
is the slider tailing away,
the believable illusion of the curveball.
Who can deny the game
its psychological and metaphysical reality?
Innings that contract and expand
for no reason found this side of mysticism,
a shutout one day, fifteen runs the next.
And a rulebook that would confound John Locke.
I love the beauty
of the well-computed average, well-placed
statistic, but then I love
the infielder knocking the ball down and recovering, rifling
a throw to first base that just beats the runner
by a step, even more.
And then that mix
of normalcy and oddness: pitchers
throwing knuckleballs and emery-boards,
.300 hitters who look like lizards, fat umpires,
trembling rookies rising to the occasion, and the perfect game
every twenty years. There is magic
in every ball that clears the fence, every fancy
defensive play. Baseball,
I would not miss what takes place
between the lines
one weekend afternoon
for a season ticket
to the world's creation.

Called on Accounta Rain

In the judgement of aficionados
the home run or strikeout
leaping catch at the fence
these are the adrenaline criteria
of what it's all about

But the game is puzzling
this year's pennant winners last next year
great players gone mediocre
yes I know
nothing in life is certain

But there are moments of such stillness
in the game
                    silence much less than silence
(like at a lynching when a black guy
stares long at a white or when
power fails during an electrocution)
and in the silence:
a hundred years have gone by
and everyone here is long dead
Reagan is dead Mulroney is dead
everyone now alive has forgotten them
until a banjo .120 hitter smacks a homer
then a great sigh from the stands
and wind roars between planets

If there really is a heaven baseball
certainly must be played there
and if there's a hell there too
and they play a universal World Series
every aeon or millenium or so
when Babe Ruth gets sick again on hot dogs
and Dizzy Dean drunk on celestial beer
Ted Williams pops up and tips his hat (sometimes)
where everything that happened keeps happening
and all that we dreamed we love
is still true when we wake up
Well if it ain't that way it oughta be
and either way there was always You
sitting next to me or in bed or somewhere
nearby while the Game goes on and on

Reliever

he strolls in from center field.
his turn to relieve.
a man in the crowd points
to the pitcher's mound
flings out advice
but the pitcher's glove catches and quietly
drops the spectator's advice on the turf.
the man, still gesturing, reminds the reliever:
keep your fastball low
don't let your curve hang
be sure your slider …
and the crowd gulps down
the man and his words.

reliever trudges to the mound slowing down
as his plan picks up tempo.
he looks up at the man
pretends to nod
warms up by tossing back at his father
those two words still caught
in the webbing of his glove.

Time Has Nothing To Do

John Donne wears a baseball cap
and a poem-filled mitt.
he can't make it to first base
with a small magazine editor.

his poems are not quite there.
they simply don't add enough
to the placid way of the nineteen seventies.

Donne warns the editor
if this were the seventeen hundreds
the editor's head would be planted
in an open field
and
all the composure in the world
wouldn't soften the influence
of the sun's fists.

Donne receives his expected sour response
saying how times are tough
and all the arrogance he could possibly muster
couldn't arm-wrestle the sun
into thinking the way he does.

Jays Win American League East, 1985

April 27, 1813:
1700 cheering American troops
from Sacket's Harbor, New York State,
land west of Little York (Toronto),
then push on for the main fort works
where the British garrison blow their grand magazine,
leaving 38 dead and 222 lying wounded;
but, undaunted, press on to capture
the town without any further trouble.

October 5, 1985:
26 road-uniformed New York Yankees
step ashore this afternoon
at old muddy York again,
and before long are met
by 26 white-uniformed
home-team Toronto Blue Jays.

This time, after nine explosive innings,
the damn Yankees are beaten at last
by the pitcher's arm, the bat,
not by any force of arms,
bloody loss of dead and dying.

Little Bat At Last Broken

for George Bowering

Yankee-made in the Adirondacks
of solid mountain ash,
black-coloured, wavy grain, very light to swing,
this bat took me through twenty seasons
of softball good and bad, and while I stuck with her
gave me very few strike-outs, many base hits
(not big hits, mind you, but the kind
most ballgames are won by).

And so today like a fool
I took this last souvenir
of so many sweat-filled, nerve-tingling innings,
along to the office game, maybe thinking what the hell
it's probably the last time you'll ever play
in anything like a real ballgame
so why not go down swinging hard
with Little Bat in your hands?

Which probably would have gone all right,
only I wasn't content with that,
had to shoot my big mouth off
about how really great my bat was,
even calling it the Ron Hunt Special,
which was a lot of BS, then made the mistake
of leaving it down with all the other bats.

So along comes some jerk, took it up to the plate,
didn't hold the label up,
and on the first pitch broke it clean in half,
with everyone on the field laughing hard but me.

And I was so mad with myself after that
I didn't even take it home with me
when the game was over, left it lying there in the park,
still beautiful somehow, still the greatest Little Bat,
only broken now in two, never to be used again,
a piece of dead wood
I couldn't stand to look at any more.

ALIX VANCE

Diamond Warrior

for Ab Ettinger

Many years had tasted winter
since we last shook pitching hands
thirty-two from the time
I had seen him throw
his right arm no longer
a fearsome catapult of fiery
fastballs or sharp breaking curves
once he would have scythed through
lineups of lunging batters

Time had balanced accounts
with this crafty hurler
leaving memories in yellowed clippings
and long lapsed conversations
of swung bats and hitters left
in swivel-hipped frustration

He the consummate moundsman
lean and with purposeful stride
had toiled on that rubber
thin line of reality
which some had used
to harsh advantage
for him it was a standard
he wore as an actor's mask

He gave himself away
in the company of animals
when he talked about fishing or
walked the quiet woods picking
wildberries on a different hill

Then the years collapsed when
I read in my distant hometown paper
his valley hands had been stilled
this poem like baseball
takes place between the lines

With closed eyes it's 1951 again
the smell of diamond dust and
cut grass magic hold my mind
like a warm June night
a time when young Ravens
were witness to his grace
while Hawks could only wait

until he got the sign
to begin the ritual windup
then delivered the final
singing pitch.

IN COMPETITION

My friends believe in golf . . .
— Alden Nowlan

Golf Lesson

for Polly

The pro's firm hands
lay a driver across her palm,
and wrap thin fingers around.
Thumbs hug inverted Vs toward ground.
Head down. . . .

Slow motion unfolds her.
Swing. . . .
Again now,
again. . . .

Arms slide back the club,
testing new faith in its arc
until wrists cock
and silver parallels earth.

Breathe!

And the arms sweep down.
— PLOCK —
A white dot climbs
its long graceful parabola
toward faint trees, the sky,

while freed by the swing's force
my daughter's whole body flows after,
opened toward flight and future.
Wrists loosen, then fall.

The circle perfected,
a first, small moon has soared
far into the next moment.

Closer—
it must be closer—
to the cup.

Golfers

Like Sieur Montaigne's distinction
between virtue and innocence
what gets you is their unbewilderment

They come into the picture suddenly
like unfinished houses, gapes and planed wood,
dominating a landscape

And you see at a glance
among sportsmen they are the metaphysicians,
intent, untalkative, pursuing Unity

(What finally gets you is their chastity)

And that no theory of pessimism is complete
which altogether ignores them

Bangor Municipal Golf Course

We talk up a thaw; the dogs
Skid on the iced sod, after a stick

As if it were baited with meat, *Chaw-chawing* it.
We retrieve the conversation:

Cost of coal, new central
Heating, bombs; the Troubles' uncalculated

Curve, all directions missed unlike the few
Golf balls, gannets dipping at the sea.

The diehards golf; clubs chatter in their bag,
Spit static like electric eels or stainless

Steel cobras. "Why don't they knock it off?" we say;

Our talk skids over the old laments on the longest
Night, the too-short days. A diehard drives

Past the pole, the yellow range-ball neutered
By the sun. "Did you see the length

On that. Boy, I'd like to smack
Off that hard top, get the bounce, lose

It altogether." The dogs drag their back
Ends after a hacked-up Ben Hogan,

Hand-thrown, hopping a hundred yards —
A gannet skipping whitecaps,

Boring into the brief mauve, hilltop
Horizon before the sky's colour thins upward

To mother-of-pearl, the ceiling
On the cold clam we're living in.

"Let me," McCloskey says,
"Just one smack."

He appeals to the diehard. The ball
Splats, stretches long through the thin

Altered air, enters another solstice
In one. The dogs heel. We talk up a thaw.

Golf

My friends believe in golf, address the ball,
however bent, to an appointed place.
Newtonians, convinced no orb can fall
out of the numbered course of time and space.

But I, from clumsiness or pity, drive
balls out of bounds and into woods and traps,
my knees and wrists vindictive in their love
for dark and tangled places not on maps.

"Golf's not your game," they say. But I persist.
"Next one goes straight ..." I promise. Oh, they're fooled
right cunningly by my secretive wrist
that treacherously lets the world go wild.

Let them attack the green. As for myself,
I pitch into the darkness, like a wolf.

Jock o' the Links

Ah Jock! I'm sure that as a right
Good honest friend I ken ye,
And damned be he that would indite
A scornful word agen' ye:
A self-controlled God-fearin' Scot,
You fight with all that's evil,
But every time you top your shot
The odds are with the devil.

A softer heart in human breast
I do not know another,
And many a time, in many a test,
You've proved yourself a brother.
That man, I'll swear, is not alive
More temperate in speech,
But every time you fan your drive
I get beyond your reach.

That God is partial to the plaid,
Long-suffering, too, I've heard;
I hope He was the day I had
You stymied on the third;
I cannot vouch for rumour, but
One thing I trust is clear,
That when He saw you miss the putt,
He turned His one deaf ear.

I'm thankful, too, that when you dub
Your spoon, it's not on me
You break your new steel-shafted club,
But on your Highland knee.
And wise I have been to abstain
From comments on your stance,
With pibrochs crashing through your brain,
Culloden through your glance.

Wrestling Ring

The inverted funnel pouring its light like alcohol
upon the Roman arch of the wheeling torsos:
stance, grapple, and grip; under their leather
muscles as big as mice: about the square,
like the sex of stallions the round taut rope:
all is vigor, mansmell, and potence.

Now, look:
See, as the favorite has the villain on the hip,
spreadeagled,
luminous with sweat, light, and pain —
the little runt in the sixth row back — a sibling? —
hop on his seat.
His small arms fill the arena; his anaemia
flows through the blue veins of the cigarette smoke;
the tatooer's needle his voice:
    Donnes-y-là! Donnes-y!
Into his seat, he drops back
exhausted.

Above the Jungle Law

He waited nervous, chafing,
To do battle with his man.
Flicked his glance ferocious
Across the mat's small span.

He flexed and coiled his muscles;
Did a little ritual dance.
This effort now was mirrored
By his enemy's simple prance.

They closed with savage caution,
And darted back like asps
A leap, A feint, A parried thrust
A lull of heaving gasps.

They circled now more wary;
Each seeking out the flaw,
To help him win this even test
And prove the jungle law.

The thing for which each fought on
Was not a life or limb,
But every wise important move
Was a victory to him.

To the rest, they fought on neutral.
Their positions changed at once.
A piercing blast of whistle
Drowned out the sick'ning crunch.

One left the mat agrimace
With a painful cradled arm.
In a jungle one must take a chance
That he will come to harm.

"Now this would swing the balance,"
The thought went through the crowd.
"He has his elbow bandaged."
(I thought, perhaps, they growled.)

But then a strange and wondrous thing
Took place before their sight.
The smooth-faced boy — uninjured —
He forsook his jungle right.

He took no vantage from the hurt
His enemy sustained,
But at his strength aligned himself
A position he maintained.

Each fought on courageous.
It ended in a draw
A tribute to the one who
Lived above the jungle law.

Bil (the throwing dummy)

You stand there unsteady on your
Single, solid, elephantine leg
Helpless unless
I hold you.
Your unidextrous underpinnings
And thalidomide arms
Are the spawn of some
Ogres sightless and mute
Capable only of fighting.
You cannot feel, smile get
Laid or excited or mad.
Implacable, inscrutable,
Unfeeling. Smooth-skinned and
Featureless as a sea creature
Your head is but a ball.
All these things I know
But I fear the latency in you.
Yesterday, in our love-hate
Struggle, I took you in my arms
And as we flew through the air
Like birds with locked wings
I felt something stir within you
And when we landed, you held me down.
I thought I saw a smile on your
Chrome-tanned, Malmo face.
I think I'll let you fall back, Bil.
You are helpless unless
I hold you.

Dressing for the Match

You pull on the clean
White tubes that
Clasp warm reassurance.
Support you crave now
Before the struggle
To soothe you like
A mother's touch to
Calm the frantic
Drumming inside that
Pushes all the air
Away so you gasp just
From bending over.

The Weigh-In

You are a pair in a line
Of nervous-pimpled
White buttocks
Like risen loaves in
A bakery of boys
Ready for the weighing
Watching with
Cornered eyes the
Tumbling numbers,
A lottery you can
Win with any digits
Under.
Feet placed precisely,
Breathing high
To lift the heaviness
Of your kneaded,
Phyllo body, you
Will the weight away
And hope.

MARK COCHRANE

Craft in the Body

You return to the game ice-cold
after nine years, & all is dreary:
air balls, fouls, jammed thumbs,
you could not buy a basket
or a decent assist. At six-foot-five
you cannot fail to rebound, but
nothing executes, your *gimme*
from two feet away
rattles around the rim
& jumps out, you catch
an elbow on the lip, split,
then pass to the other team
in a panic, till shame starts to sap
the blood of every shot
short.
        But a moment comes,
you have resigned yourself
& fatigue's got you delirious,
faking it, a jogger running empty
laps of the court, when you
scoop in an alley-oop
along the end line,
take it down
totally without thinking,
& (stepping over a guard, his
planted knee) you circle
the ball around your hips,
charge beneath
& lay it up thru the backdoor,
the spin you put on the seams
squeaking the glass —

& that bite of the leather
is what does it, drives the wedged
orange, laterally, into the strings
& still you have not
even looked up, the guys all
laughing & slapping your shoulders, they
accuse you of holding back

until now, when the phantom
boy within you, his very lineaments
sketched in the strands
of your old neurons,
roused up
& spoke in the supple
language of his wrist & yours,
This is what we remember.

Winter Ball

The squat man under the hoop
throws in short hooks, left-handed, right
in the dwindling sunlight as six lesbians
clown and shoot at the other end,
through a very loose game of three on three.

How pleased to be among themselves,
warm New Year's Day afternoon, neither young
nor graceful nor really good shots
but happy for the moment while a mutt
belonging to one of them runs

nearly out of its skin so glad to be
near the action and smells, vigorous and dumb
but keeping his orbits well-clear of the man
who would be a machine now if he could,
angling them in off both sides of the backboard.

You can tell this is a thing he's often done,
the boy who'd shoot till dusk
when starlings exploded, filthy birds,
from roost to roost, gathering only to fly off
at the first sharp sound, hundreds as one.

He'd wonder where they went at night
as he played his solitary game of *Round the World*,
sinking shots from along the perimeter,
then the lay-up, then the foul.
So intent at it
and grave it almost seemed like more than a game
with dark coming on and the cold.

Right-Handed Hook Shot, 15 Feet Out

Again in the gym like
eager mornings, kicking through leaves
pushing oak doors open and
sunlight holy on blond wood

Leap, hoop, ball's rough pebbles
in fingerflex and the hinge
of my wrist, a tomtom against the squeal
of sneakers, pimples
and the short sweet skirts of cheerleaders
everything measured by the scoreboard.

No longer that apple-innocence
twenty years later in the dank
green meanness of the hospital gym
hacking and fumbling after five
minutes, the patients ignoring
rules and charging all
around me elbows and knees.

When I snag a high pass
they're on me like flies
a quick feint to lose
one, turn right and drive
towards the pockmarked backboard
like the ball was tied to my hand
one man left, playing deep.   I fake

a shot and turn
right, jumping high and my
arm curves like I was
holding a woman or the whole
goddam world   just the right
backspin to soften the arc
over his outstretched arms like it had eyes
spurning the backboard dropping clean
through the hoop out the torn net
we take them by two points.

Sundown at Fletcher's Field

Ruder light was taken by sail
to the bishop of Seville
than this benison
suddenly on us like oil
pressed warm from olives.

The west goal mouth
is free for an instant but the kick
is high. Two wings
in green shorts cry out.

But the ball stays up. The sun
on its way down
has swallowed the world.
The park's suffused,

the shirts and the dogs,
with the burnish of Corelli's horns.

DOROTHY LIVESAY

Soccer Game

O early let the ball
spin early O
and fall
through thin-spun misty air
right to the goalie's hug.

And bounce it once
hard to the ground
sharp, vicious kick
and beat
beat back again
into the sea of knees
the pounding field.

O let the ball be
lightsome, curl of light
tossed as a halo
head to head
knocked as a message knocks
between two men
who wheel and spin
manoeuvring
feet   head
            head   feet
but hands forever tied
unless "offside"
and on to sidelines
hugged to breast
round world, bounced
and then released.

And once again
into the melee, each
man tied to each
his shadow
dodging him
bogging and stopping him
round
round the field a dance
to the ball's bounce

        Until a sudden huddle
        waffles it
        between fast feet —
        the toe's a needle
                quivering
        towards the net —

ball circles   soars
and lunging
it is plunged
straight to the win

The crowd roars!
(but only the clock
has won).

A Sporting Life

In a green field on Easter Day,
Jesus rises up among the soccer players;
in the stands people hold
coarse hotdogs, their jobs, celestial navigation, swallowing
the afternoon like an industry.
Jesus begins to speak, about the Liquor Commission,
so many cases of domestic wine;
a famous forward kicks passes around him.
Meanwhile, past the stand, someone thinks about ham
for dinner, garnished with pineapple.
Others sit in a hotel lobby, near the radio,
arguing about lotteries. A sign at their back says:
No noise after this hour.

Around the world, new colloquialisms
are accepted into the language.
I record them with a bad accent,
ill at ease & out of ammo.
Even history books invent fresh causes, sources, continually
reasonable men.
What the facts show at a given hour.
One acts; one acts; never enough
money, too many milkshake cures.

In the green field of afternoon, Jesus.
Risen among the soccer players, finance companies, skewered wieners.
He wants to play, but no one lets him; they call for
evidence, & a set of statutes.
Like refrigerators, ministers, lawyers risen from the universities.
Opposition leaders decrying *the worst government
in history.*
So he turns from the field, Jesus, alone
because the game is not over, & walks
to the Acropol, which he likes; & he sits for hours
beneath its liquor license, the rows of
glasses, the statue
of his blue mother   among the bottles behind the bar

MILTON ACORN

The Fights

What an elusive target
the brain is! Set up
like a coconut on a flexible stem
it has 101 evasions.
A twisted nod slews a punch
a thin gillette's width
past a brain, or
a rude brush-cut to the chin
tucks one brain safe under another.
Two of these targets are
set up to be knocked down
for 25 dollars or a million.

In that TV picture in the parlor
the men, tho linked move to move
in a chancy dance,
are abstractions only.
Come to ringside, with two
experts in there! See
each step or blow pivoted,
balanced and sudden as gunfire.
See muscles wriggle, shine
in sweat like windshield rain.

In stinking dancehalls, in
the forums of small towns,
punches are cheaper but
still pieces of death.
For the brain's the target
with its hungers
and code of honor. See
in those stinking little towns,
with long counts, swindling judges,
how fury ends with the last gong.
No matter who's the cheated one
they hug like a girl and man.

It's craft and
the body rhythmic and terrible,
the game of struggle.
We need something of its nature
but not this;
for the brain's the target
and round by round it's whittled
til nothing's left of a man
but a jerky bum, humming
with a gentleness less than human.

Boxing On Europe's Most Beautiful Beach

A slow breeze north from Africa
would not allow the surf to chill
our modest vinho, up
to its neck in sand, on time
to wash down heavy farm rolls
and oleaginating cheese-of-the-hills.

She surprised me, as bantam-weights
can do, with a neat left cross
to the side of the head
and thought to make a combination
with a straight right hand.

I ducked. At my back an igneous
bluff loomed burnt-sienna.
What was I to do? I counter-
punched, just above the elastic
waist of her skyblue underpants.
Down she went, doubled
like an embryo in sand.

Her arm raised to shield
her eyes from the winter sun
or me, was dark, the flesh mingling
nicely with the abundant strands
of down from her wrist to elbow.

        Her breasts,
like troubled engines, rose
and fell as she worked to find
her breath. Her face, as soft
in line as any Burne-Jones painted
except for the gag-tooth
and chin, a trifle Slovak,
changed from a pellucid blue
to red to the kind of pink
uncommon but for the magnolia.
Reluctant to turn away,
though courtesy required it,
I brought the wine and rolls.
Is reciprocity not the kernel
of all Confucius taught? So when
she knocked the tendered cup
out of my hand, hope for perfect
accord spilt there too. And yet,
with unmistakable sweetness,
she did say,
            Hit me again.

Plato's Bonspiel

for Bob McBain

On the middle sheet
Of the Academy C.C.
Socrates, the persuasive skip
Holds the broom for Glaucon
In the hack, ready
To be guided.

The double raise through a port
The angle raise takeout
The hit and roll across the house to cover
and backing
The perfect freeze
Each as the Forms dictate.

End after end
Rock follows rock, all on line
All possible shots made
In dull perfection.

The Bonspiel Song

oh, I went to the bonspiel to have a little fun
got me a room and a little jug of rum
now I set that jug in the corner of the rink
everytime I shot, I'd take a little drink

the jug got low, I got high
tried to play a guard but I laid her by
got her up and down and I took out our own
the skip hollers up, "why don't ya go home"

this curling sure is a slippery game
I think I'd do better if I didn't take aim
I shoot for the broom but I hit both sides
I think I must be a getting cross-eyed

skip hollers in, I throw an out
we're down near the end and he calls me out
then he comes up, lets a runner go
takes out three rocks but they're all our own

when the game is over we hobble off the ice
my knee feels like it needs a splice
we go and have lunch and I must say
those ladies deserve a lot of praise

there's coffee and sandwiches, pie and cake
makes you forget that shot you didn't make
you'll never know how good you can feel
until you've curled in the ol' bonspiel

107. The Hamilton Tiger-Cats

As we registered I asked the guy about boats. I thought it would be a good idea to take the kids fishing in the morning. When I was a kid my dad and my uncles used to take me fishing a lot. My kids had never gone fishing. The proprietor said the boat and motor would be twelve bucks. Canoes were three bucks an hour. As for fishing gear, he didn't rent it. "I've never had any call for it," he said.

It turned out the guy was a refugee from Hamilton, Ont. When he saw me writing Hamilton on the registration form he said, "How is that smoky, polluted city?"

"Terrible," I said. "We get away from it every chance we can." It's simpler than trying to explain why you like it.

"I used to live there," said the guy. "I was born and raised there." He looked like Vladimir Nabokov and had a shining bald spot on his head.

His wife came up and started smiling. She was about fifty, quite lovely. Even the numerous liver spots on her face were charmingly arranged.

"Are you from Hamilton too?" I said.

"I was born in Toronto actually," she said, "but I lived most of my life in Hamilton."

"You're smart. You got out."

"Oh, I don't know. We quite like it. We still go back quite a bit. Tiger-Cats aren't doing so well this year are they?"

Half Time Parade

Into the centre of the football field

the Americans are spreading themselves out

again

Five hundred marching men
ten girls
and three or four seals

the band fills every corner
of the
other half of their continent

(and overflows into
my living room)

the cameraman
veers away from the noise

the picture slants
but there's no escape

focussing on the sky
            (cloudless jetted)
he is overpowered by drums
shoots into the crowd
aimlessly

all the scrubbed young eyes
are mesmerized
the flags are flown
the boots click
(it is Nuremberg
or Rome)

waving the camera
unreleased
(the picture whirls)
the cameraman gives in
sets his frozen eyes
hard upon the glitter
(failing to notice the babies
wailing in the upper stands
or the popcorn boy
grown grey haired and unintelligible.)

Tennis

Service is joy, to see or swing. Allow
All tumult to subside. Then tensest winds
Buffet, brace, viol and sweeping bow.
Courts are for love and volley. No one minds
The cruel ellipse of service and return,
Dancing white galliardes at tape or net
Till point, on the wire's tip, or the long burn-
ing arc to nethercourt marks game and set.
Purpose apart, perched like an umpire, dozes,
Dreams golden balls whirring through indigo.
Clay blurs the whitewash but day still encloses
The albinos, bonded in their flick and flow.
Playing in musicked gravity, the pair
Score liquid Euclids in foolscaps of air.

GEORGE McWHIRTER

Ace

Between two stalks of tall
Grass, another web, strung
On loose strands like the mesh
Of a tired tennis racquet,

Sags with the chill delivery
Of dew

And light. Sad white sun,
It can never volley you back
To the height

Of June,
Those indelible blue solitudes.

Safety

Far off in the washroom, the light comes thru, the sound
of him throwing up dinner,
his sickness,
his body so hard it won't digest,
won't welcome food
In the newspaper, a picture of Gilles Villeneuve
in the last second of his life,
his car already demolished,
his body in the air
turned-over
about to slam its bones into the wall
So many kilometres per hour,
with or without the Ferrari.
& the small man in the washroom, who admires
but will not listen
to the fast man who says death is boring.
I can't drive slower, he says.
I drive at my limits, for
the pleasure, purely

& you, in this house, listening to the small man's body
turn over its cylinders,
refusing its food
What part you play here, the pattern,
the man sick with alcohol,
who wants boredom,
who wants to be a dead man in your arms'
bent safety without cure
or derision
the way Villeneuve held his body in the air,
so fast only the camera stopped him

Bocce Players, September

The moon's out to help
the *bocce* players tonight,
but all they really need
is the one light thrown
from the school's second storey
to the tennis-court below,

where these friends, these neighbours,
take wondrous, impossible shots,
coax lovingly clicking balls,
four shadowed figures caught
and held in the darkness,
not wanting to start what they know
will be the last game of the year.

"Marry a *bocce* player
and see him only
when the snow falls."

Maybe the Italians
never had this saying.
Well, they have it now.

Mother of the Lacrosse Goalie

Tonight is the big game. Kevin is nervous, misses the "soft" ones. (Mothers learn this language slowly. Kevin has explained the terminology, patiently, more than once.)

His team can only afford the second-best pads. Last week a ball hit his head and he toppled neatly, all six-foot-five of him, straight as any soldier, in slow motion descent. The crack of his helmet on the cement floor was like a rifle shot in the suddenly quiet arena. Later, when both teams began to brawl, my son was an innocent hostage. The only reason I didn't rush to battle to save him was his father, holding me physically to my seat. *Just part of the game*, he insisted.

Tonight as this game pounds on, Kevin is "uneven" (This is his father's term. I think it means playing well for 5 minutes, fading for 10.) In the end, his team loses.

At breakfast the next morning we sit at the kitchen table, in my territory now. *You seemed nervous last night*, I say. He shrugs. This is what goalies do.

When you feel anxious, I tell him, *you need a strategy. What I have learned is to pretend I am a tree.* (Ignore his raised eyebrows. This is important. It took years to learn this.) *I pretend my roots are going deep in the earth, holding me steady. Then I am ready for anything, can handle anything.*

There is a moment's pause. He grins. *I know what you mean, Mom*, he says. *You do?* I'm amazed he catches on so quickly, this clever child. *Yeah, about strategy. I come out of the net and hit somebody.*

Hit? I repeat stupidly.

Yeah, on the back of the legs, or yell at the ref. It's connection, Mom. You make connection. Isn't that what you mean?

Is it? This child of streetfights and temper tantrums, of soft teddy bears and hugs. This child who embraces the whole world with his body. All of it. Over and over he has explained to me that when you are big, as he is, people pick on you as a test. Of themselves. *This is what boys do*, he says to me, over and over when I can't understand it, when it is different for girls. This manchild has learned, if not from me, to touch others, not always gently. To make the connection physical.

His face now is alight, waiting. *Yes*, I nod. *That's it. In our own way, we all have a strategy. In our own way, we all make connection.*

TRONI Y. GRANDE

For Antigone, Excluded from Sand-Volleyball

Born to oppose
The daughter revives
Ninth-life pleas
Let me in
The game!

Your blood
Your mouth roars in vein and artery
Black male fuelled with revenge
Against the sky you loom
The game is not for losers
The game is man's alone
Us Them
Launch the Blitzkrieg
Vergeltungswaffe finds its mark
O bully for you!
Ninth-hour scarlet
And enemies will be
Of the self-same household

Hence this retreat
My sidelines role
Though not without power
Triumphant volley
Strategic service

I lie watchfully
Waiting on truth
That certain moment when
Fumbling the serve
Your feet will stumble
Buried you think in the dignity of sand
But covered I know in catshit

LONE FIGURES

If she climbs from the pool
will she become an ordinary woman …
— Lorna Crozier

Younger Sister, Going Swimming

Northern Quebec

Beside this lake
where there are no other people

my sister in bathing suit continues
her short desolate
parade to the end of the dock;

against the boards
her feet make sad statements
she thinks no one can hear;

(I sit in a deckchair
not counting, invisible;
the sun wavers on
this page as on a pool.)

She moves the raft out
past the sandy point;
no one comes by in a motorboat.

She would like to fill the lake
with other swimmers, with answers.
She calls her name. The sun encloses
rocks, trees, her feet in the water, the circling
bays and hills as before.

She poises, raises her arms
as though signalling, then disappears.
The lake heals itself quietly
of the wound left by the diver.
The air quakes and is still.

(Under my hand the paper
closes over these
marks I am making on it.

The words ripple, subside,
move outwards toward the shore.)

The Swimmer's Moment

For everyone
The swimmer's moment at the whirlpool comes,
But many at that moment will not say
"This is the whirlpool, then."
By their refusal they are saved
From the black pit, and also from contesting
The deadly rapids, and emerging in
The mysterious, and more ample, further waters.
And so their bland-blank faces turn and turn
Pale and forever on the rim of suction
They will not recognize.
Of those who dare the knowledge
Many are whirled into the ominous centre
That, gaping vertical, seals up
For them an eternal boon of privacy,
So that we turn away from their defeat
With a despair, not from their deaths, but for
Ourselves, who cannot penetrate their secret
Nor even guess at the anonymous breadth
Where one or two have won:
(The silver reaches of the estuary).

The Swimmer

In the solarium pool
she separates like milk
into what is heavy and what is not,
splits like sunlight
passed through a prism.

On the bottom,
dolphin-grey and graceful
her shadow swims.
Eyes closed,
it knows only one thing,
something she can't articulate
but it has to do with motion.

On the ceiling made of glass
her reflection looks back at her,
not with recognition
but with slight surprise
as her head, arms and legs
form the five points of a star.

In between, the part of her
that feels the warmth of water,
her muscles' stretch and pull,
repeats the strokes
she learned as a child.

She wonders how she'll bring
these parts back together.
If she climbs from the pool
will she become an ordinary woman
with children waiting, her darkness
folded like a scarf and tucked away,
her reflection moving to the bathroom mirror?

She hesitates to swim to the ladder,
feel the steel rungs
press against her soles. Maybe
this is how a woman drowns,
raising her arm three times,
not a call for help
but a gesture of acknowledgement,
of recognition

as she becomes one
with her body,
one with her shadow,
one with her drifting star.

H. C. DILLOW

Child Swimming in the Ramapo

Rising from the green pattern of his vision,
He breaks the surface and is shown forth
To the splayed birches at the river's edge,
Shouts and is proclaimed to the attentive air,
Fathers the gaudy sunfish, is himself
Warmly sired in the sun's salacious eye
And figures to flight with his curious gaze
The ponderous crow. Heels down and firmly
Planted in the bottom's ooze, eye-level with
The water-skaters' shifting constellations,
He rocks idly to summer's voices —
Bluebottle, gnat, peripatetic bee —
Sounding in his ear like golden horns
And listens for the first time to the living
Ground bass of the one unutterable poem.

A Real Pro

I went to college with George Young,
who was world famous for swimming
from Los Angeles to Catalina Island
and later in Lake Ontario off the Toronto
Exhibition Park   I was a good-enough swimmer
that I didn't take any lessons in a course
at Varsity   I merely went out for the final examination
and was told to dive into the pool, swim over
and rescue that man   So I did all that
towing the man with one arm crooked around his neck
Then we both stood up before the examiner
(I passed)   I noticed that the man I'd rescued was
  George Young
After he turned away from standing beside me
before the examiner, the great famous George Young
went over behind a stone column in Hart House
and vomited
          Later my sea-god told me
"you nearly drowned me   When you towed me,
you had my mouth and nose under water"
But before he let go of that water, this pro
had stood beside me before the examiner,
his eyeballs must have been floating
— a real pro

Endurance

for J.H.

— at the crack she pounced
hours over the grip of pool, she split
the skin and scythed like a lover back

to breast the surface, rush with fluid
motion towards a standing wall; she coiled,
sprang, and her back broke

water, fin-slick, arched again and drove.
Someday the water's skin will not give,
its flesh will stiffen around her, gathering

strands of her hair and strength, then burrow
her down like a loon through pools
of calm. Her crawl will slacken but find in rest

the power of sea-beds, mussels, coral,
that work in the rhythms of sleep a pearl
of flesh. See her flail with brief endurance:

when the race ends, there is still this.

The Diver

Like marble, nude, against the purple sky,
In ready poise, the diver scans the sea,
Gemming the marsh's green placidity
And mirroring the fearless form on high.
Behold the outward leap — he seems to fly!
His arms like arrow-blade just speeded free;
His body like the curving bolt, to be
Deep driven till the piercing flight shall die.
Sharply the human arrow cleaves the tide,
Only a foaming swell to mark his flight;
While shoreward moves the silent ring on ring.
And now the sea is stirred and broken wide
Before the swimmer's passage free and light,
And bears him as a courser bears a king.

Lone Bather

Upon the ecstatic diving board the diver,
poised for parabolas, lets go
lets go his manshape to become a bird.
Is bird, and topsy-turvy
the pool floats overhead, and the white tiles snow
their crazy hexagons. Is dolphin. Then
is plant with lilies bursting from his heels.

Himself, suddenly mysterious and marine,
bobs up a merman leaning on his hills.
Splashes and plays alone the deserted pool;
as those, is free, who think themselves unseen.
He rolls in his heap of fruit,
he slides his belly over
the melonrinds of water, curved and smooth and green.
Feels good: and trains, like little acrobats
his echoes dropping from the galleries;
circles himself over a rung of water;
swims fancy and gay; taking a notion, hides
under the satins of his great big bed, —
and then comes up to float until he thinks
the ceiling at his brow, and nowhere any sides.

His thighs are a shoal of fishes: scattered: he
turns with many gloves of greeting
towards the sunnier water and the tiles.

Upon the tiles he dangles from his toes
lazily the eight reins of his ponies.

An afternoon, far from the world
a street sound throws like a stone, with paper, through the glass.
Up, he is chipped enamel, grained with hair.
The gloss of his footsteps follows him to the showers,
the showers, and the male room, and the towel
which rubs the bird, the plant, the dolphin back again
personable plain.

IRVING LAYTON

The Breaststroke

May the gods be praised that I should meet
on my final lap to the eternal sea
one so young, so gracious and lovely,
under clear skies promising as herself.
Ankled deep in the scorching sands
I can hear the shouting tide; in it
invitation and menace like the smile
on the fair face of my companion,
making me wish to nuzzle forever
between her firm thighs and cover
her mouth with long hungering kisses.

Insensate to everything but her warm flesh
I'd float out into the voluptuous sea,
my practised breaststroke perfect at last.
The heaving mounds pressed against me,
alluring me past the white wavecrests
that close behind like tall portals
barring return. Green towers collapse
on bright medallions larger than suns;
the virginal foam breaks into bridal cries
and after the last loud crash of savaging breasts,
into the long silence that no man hears.

The Swimmer

The afternoon foreclosing, see
The swimmer plunges from his raft,
Opening the spray corollas by his act of war —
The snake heads strike
Quickly and are silent.

Emerging see how for a moment,
A brown weed with marvellous bulbs,
He lies imminent upon the water
While light and sound come with a sharp passion
From the gonad sea around the poles
And break in bright cockle-shells about his ears.

He dives, floats, goes under like a thief
Where his blood sings to the tiger shadows
In the scentless greenery that leads him home,
A male salmon down fretted stairways
Through underwater slums. . . .

Stunned by the memory of lost gills
He frames gestures of self-absorption
Upon the skull-like beach;
Observes with instigated eyes
The sun that empties itself upon the water,
And the last wave romping in
To throw its boyhood on the marble sand.

First Dive

Shivering in the hot August sun
   I stand on the lowest diving board
watching above me the giants
fearlessly twist and knife
into their dark waters

I measure distance
in terms of
multiple whales
and weigh my eleven years
against the terrors
circulating quietly and steadily
under the surface
the eyes that stare from green rocks
at my naked feet
the hands weaving seaweed nets
to complete the ambiguity
of my needless capture
a surfeit of teeth and claws gathering
to oversee my fate

Reckless with fear
I become a wavering sigh
   a reluctant bird
lose head and hands and atmosphere
to trespass suddenly
into adult depths
bobbing up   transfigured   victorious
out of an unclaimed ocean.

Proust in the Waters

for Scott and Krystyne

Swimming along the bar of moon
the yellow scattered sleeping
arm of the moon
                    on Balsam Lake

releasing the air
                    out of your mouth
the moon under your arm
tick of the brain
submerged. Tick
of the loon's heart
in the wet night thunder
                         below us
knowing its shore is the air

We love things which disappear
and are found
creatures who plummet
and become
an arrow.
To know the syllables
in a loon sentence
                    intricate
shift of preposition
that signals meridian
                      west   south west
The mother tongue
a bubble caught in my beak
releasing the air
                    of a language

Seeing no human in this moon storm
being naked in black water
you approach the corridor
such jewellery! Queen Anne's Lace!
and slide to fathoms, androgynous.
The mouth swallows river morse
throws a sound
through the loom of liquid
against sky.

                        Where are you?

On the edge
of the moon bar

The Snorkler

Arrayed in fins and goggles
the cloven creature, genius
of division, stands
gawkily upon the shore
making up his fractured mind
which way to move, or whether
to stand a minute more

surveying first the sea, not
for sharks or jellyfish
or bone-scraping rocks, but
an indefinable threat
that marrow-jelling cold
and elemental blue
evoke: part fear and part regret

to trouble his propriety;
or turn and through his glass
(which both clouds and magnifies)
observe the raven-mortised sky
close above him, the cliff
at the sea's back, vaulted in air,
and, as if to signify

the natal mystery
of merely being what it is,
the thing itself in its
appointed place, the sun blares
in his temples, fire-trumpet.
It's the declamatory
pride nature shares

with everything that is not
plural. Which is his element
who can accomodate them all
by bartering his grace
for that ungainly
versatility, his sense
of being and of place

to be at home in
anything but his rifted self?
He adjusts the rubber tube,
so queerly umbilical,
stressing a primitive
dependence on some placental
element, though alien still,

and treading awkwardly,
with a kind of flippant
inappropriate air,
he frog-flops in a width
of sea, all thrashings and snorts,
and snorkles clumsily
beyond his necessary depth.

Marathon Swimmers

That summer our family boarded out at the Rogers'
Hanlan's Point cottage. As it was a two-week holiday
I must have seen Martha, their seventeen-year-old daughter,
at least fourteen times (her body when I saw it
in its black bathing-suit looked much, much older to me),
either heading out the front door in the early morning
to start her five-mile training swim, or coming back later
dripping wet with a bathrobe around her,
hair every which way after being under her bathing-cap.

Her father as trainer was strictly no-nonsense
(one stormy day I heard him tell his wife
"We had to quit after only two miles because she kept stopping
to throw up"). So morning after summer morning
Martha's red bathing-cap kept bobbing up
fifty yards from shore with her father sculling after
in a rowboat. (It was one of the years
of the big Exhibition marathon swims, magic events
leading on to fame and fortune each fall,
everyone of course set on being another George Young,
though George hadn't done very much
since his great Catalina Island win.)

So Martha kept stroking thirty-five to the minute,
eating thick steaks and all the food
we never saw at mealtimes, and I never once managed
more than a "Good morning" to her, me the shy boy
shrivelling up at the sight of his goddess.
Then our two-week holiday ended, we came back home
to Colbeck Street and the last of the heat-heavy days.
A month later Exhibition time finally came.
First the men's swim was run, then the women's
I read the evening paper extra carefully
looking for Martha's name among the winners,
but never found it anywhere.

I suppose for the Rogers family it was just one more
in a long string of defeats life had handed them.
Perhaps after that, I thought, her red bathing-cap
wouldn't have to bob up and down, mouth choked with vomit,
and Martha could become more like a girl again,
swim in the blue lake-water like a carefree fish
only when she cared to. . . .

Woman Skating

A lake sunken among
cedar and black spruce hills;
late afternoon.

On the ice a woman skating,
jacket sudden
red against the white,

concentrating on moving
in perfect circles.

> (actually she is my mother, she is
> over at the outdoor skating rink
> near the cemetery. On three sides
> of her there are streets of brown
> brick houses; cars go by; on the
> fourth side is the park building.
> The snow banked around the rink
> is grey with soot. She never skates
> here. She's wearing a sweater and
> faded maroon earmuffs, she has
> taken off her gloves)

Now near the horizon
the enlarged pink sun swings down.
Soon it will be zero.

With arms wide the skater
turns, leaving her breath like a diver's
trail of bubbles.

Seeing the ice
as what it is, water:
seeing the months
as they are, the years
in sequence occuring
underfoot, watching
the miniature human
figure balanced on steel
needles (those compasses
floated in saucers) on time
sustained, above
time circling: miracle

Over all I place
a glass bell

Maggie T Goes Public

Maggie T
laces up her skates
& without plastic guards
tip toes to
the limo
& is driven
to the
frozen
canals
snaking thru
Ottawa
The driver waits in the car
forever as she
whirls below
the gray
sky —
each moment of life
vanishing into
the brisk
air
She is transformed
shaped into
whatever fantasy
grips 20 million
Canadians
She is public fantasy
a taxpayer's
kinky
write
off

Skating

SS No. 12
red box at the
dead-centre of our
twelve-year world

In front of the school
the pine tree (alone)
welcomed us all
in its ample crotch
(the girls, luckier,
locked it
in their own)

Ronnie Young
licked the moon
with his dry tongue

Grace Leckie, unaware,
grew breasts, we
coaxed them out of wool

From the bush
I see the plough
thrust and turn
the clay's iron
burns brown
gives up
grubs the sun
feeds on
furrows fall away in
wide thighs the
moon will sleep in

"We come from clay,"
the teacher said
(she said it for the Bible)
but I think of
dry fields/the
yielding heat

(and what is under
those brown udders of
earth the plough turns?
stubble of bull
thistle fireweed
wild mustard blue-devil
come together

for what dark
ignition?)

But cold came
held our heat under
held it in

We thought of
the red furnace
giving us
wrinkled warmth
from the belly
of the school,
throbbing below us
scarlet and obscene

In the schoolyard
we spun circles
in the snow:
"Fox and the Goose" till
the grass gleamed:
freshly dead

Overnight the
ponds became
moments of ice
we turned on the
blades of our blood
balanced on ice
between earth's unturning
and sun without power
we gathered the
strength of speed
the ice gave us
space gave
us time
was articulate
in our bone-
motion over
ice giving us
range beyond the
schoolyards of our
bodies we coasted
like kites
on the loose
when ice was our

wind gathering
in its wake

one red schoolhouse
a leering furnace
a pine-tree with a hard-on
a dozen dead geese
a pair of virgin-wool breasts
a ravenous sun
Ronnie Young's moon

thanks to
ice that
gave us breath
gave us heat
we all gave back
before the kitestrings
snapped, drew
us invisibly down
to the mothering box
at the dead-centre
of our brave and winded
red-beating
twelve-year world.

Family Pond

On the ice generations twist and writhe
small boys lash their Christmas pucks
and gallop relentlessly away from parents
agonizing
near the snowy borders
of the pond
Grandparents
conscious of the semi-circle
of stares
move in smaller and smaller arcs
and are lost to view
At this perfect moment
we emerge
clear anomalies
mysteriously shearing the ice
in no predestined
direction
oblivious of any need
to race
or cling
warmed by eyes and hands blossoming
unhampered
in a winter
we are only gliding over.

Skating

The ice booms with colour
we skate out to join the cars
climbing like small moons
over the hills
there is a whole night frozen
in front of us
the trees vacant with paralysis
but we are given time
to veer and dip
in new patterns
accepting with
joy
the tenuous connection
of the night
your eyes brush against mine
your hands promise
a selection of miracles
I who had disappeared like
yesterday's sun
cohere again
before a new unreality
turned in a series of silver grins
my life changing (innocent and parallel)
in childlike directions.

Advice To A Young Skater

The best spells
are the simplest
providing they pack
(like the long

scarf crammed
in your short sleeve)
the farthest ends
into their simplicity.

As a scatter of common salt
over the shoulder
thwarts the devil's
intricate pitchfork;

as lifting one foot
after the other
in invisible pattern
to a clapped rhythm

brings down cloudbursts
from a clear heaven —
or from an obscure one
you fetch God's ear

with tight-pressed palms,
eyes shut, as if
preparing to dive
into a glitter;

so pull the laces
tight, eyelet after eyelet,
your trapped feet
coffined in leather,

that you may float
through the best
resurrection
we can get,

not walking on water
but, arms in air,
flying over
its astonished glare.

CHARLES G. D. ROBERTS

The Skater

My glad feet shod with the glittering steel
I was the god of the winged heel.

The hills in the far white sky were lost;
The world lay still in the wide white frost;

And the woods hung hushed in their long white dream
by the ghostly, glimmering, ice-blue stream.

Here was a pathway, smooth like glass,
Where I and the wandering wind might pass

To the far-off palaces, drifted deep,
Where Winter's retinue rests in sleep.

I followed the lure I fled like a bird,
Till the startled hollows awoke and heard

A spinning whisper, a sibilant twang,
As the stroke of the steel on the tense ice rang;

And the wandering wind was left behind
As faster, faster I followed my mind;

Till the blood sang high in my eager brain,
And the joy of my flight was almost pain.

Then I stayed the rush of my eager speed
And silently went as a drifting seed, —

Slowly, furtively, till my eyes
Grew big with the awe of a dim surmise,

And the hair of my neck began to creep
At hearing the wilderness talk in sleep.

Shapes in the fir-gloom drifted near.
In the deep of my heart I heard my fear;

And I turned and fled, like a soul pursued,
From the white, inviolate solitude.

Surfaces

The hollow scrape of blades
moves skaters through crisp air
this cold, a particular winter
of toques and scarves and gloves
as superfluous as buttons
Jackets flap in the wind
of our movements

So many trajectories
a community singing on ice
the lake almost large enough, people make space
pucks and sticks
pause for these wobbly legs to pass
and no one points to laugh
The only borders here
are where lifeguards hack at the ice
check for thickness and rope off
spots too thin for safety.

We slide or glide or stumble
away from treacherous areas
into indiscriminate welcomes
to all who venture onto the lake
this surface beneath our feet
the only skin of concern

In the centre of a city
echoes of unhurried sound
take me back to the Tantramar
redwings in the rushes
their harmonica call a microcosm
of what I miss

What is it about place that seeps
into your soul
mindless of miles, however far you move —
plays out the string and holds you
tempts a false nostalgia
I catch myself believing
this momentary release from rancour
holds the possibility of a city
reclining into country life, as if back home
there was never anything like a frozen pond
abandoned to power, boys
claiming ownership of the top, slap shots
tripping girls' attempts at circles …

At some point every conversation
comments on the relief
of outdoor skating: no one dictating
now to the right, the left,
backward only, just couples,
muzak piping out the pace

Our music is disparate voices
mingled with the language of blackbirds
ducks and crows, our patterns as random
and predictable as their flight
Wings slant and turn snug in the sky
feet sculpt curves and crossroads into ice

Such a freeze is rare here — the need
to get to the middle, irresistible
just to see what it's like to look
at the path from the lake for a change
searching for perspective, almost everyone
explores the iced-in cattails and reeds
where the heron hunts when it's water
where we turn from relics of summer
locked in the frozen surface:
styrofoam, cellophane, plastic trash,
lost tennis balls and toys

we look without seeing
how fragile our smiles
when it's youths who feel free
to nod to the aged
whites to the black or the brown
then skate or stroll away
from subtle assumptions behind
who welcomes who

we sing in the same
clutches and gaggles as ever
leaving implications, like litter
for someone else to face

Cadenza

Trees shake gentle skaters out
On the arena of my sleep,
Silent colours turn and grow
On the surface of the night
Where red by red is multiplied
And blue divides its blue with ice,
And flying music lifts the edge
From tightly nailed memory.

Skaters turn and dancers whirl
In flashing curves, and voices lift
The heavy rafters of my sleep
With spiralled shouts that coalesce
And rocket skywards, close on stars —
Their sharp points cut a jagged line
Into the careful shape of peace;
Then colour captures spring
And I wake prisoner
In morning's branches.

DAVID ARNASON

The Joggers

Legs pumping, the heart
ridiculous in its exertions
we circle the concrete track.
Outside, the arterial clog
of traffic wafts white plumes
of exhaust in still winter air.
We yearn backward in time
forward to a finish line
of our own making. Intense,
we count and forget our laps,
listen to the coursing of blood
in veins we are not usually
aware of, discover the ticking
of organs whose names we know
but not their places. Backwards
we run toward some vanished
vision of perfectibility
to some lost innocence.
Alone on the crowded track
we jostle and grunt, finding
a pain that is sweeter than sackcloth
or ashes. The sweet messy
clockwork of our bodies
counting out rhymes that become
more meaningless with every shapely round.
Until, and when it's over
it is always less than we expected,
we round that final curve
to our lonesome victories
our garland of sweaty laurels
and purification by water.
Then with virtuous limps
and muscles stretched by holy
yearning we put on our other
lesser selves with our parkas
and overshoes, and enter,
a little taller, that other
amorphous world where we are not
separate from things.

Running

and you
stay beside me
as though chosen
to sing a spirit song

let the others go ahead
I only want to hear
your song in my ear

they tire while
my step lengthens

I run faster   faster
deer   spirit   pities   carries
me   deer   swift   free

my feet scarcely touch the earth
I leave behind all others
and you, partner
where are you

The Runner

Not to stutter the amnesia of the chest
while the body is still running!
Not to stutter now or the amnesia will close,
close up its forgotten chest
& the alphabet will stop its tumbling
The amnesia in which everything awakes like a soft
tread of the running figure.
Who knows this woman?
Who knows her breast is full of remembered water!
Who knows what her chest will say to us if only
it keeps up its terrible running …

Don't stop, now, chest …
Chest that touches no one …

Listen …

Circle of the Runner

from the painting by Masea Maeda

His face in shadow and turned
away, the man is running
inside a thin black circle.
One foot is raised and his arms are pumping.
Not a race, that others
go faster, last longer.
Neither to nor from
although sometimes he feels like the hour hand
of a clock, or a pet for some god.
It will never be over and he cannot stop or stand.

Even in dreams his legs jerk, fists
clench to hit against softness.
Women and women and women
aimed for the finish line
so many memories fallen under his feet,
his hands too tight for a torch or baton.

Does he bring a message

He runs into the whiteness
between himself and the circle.
Times he slows down
sucks hot air to his lungs
the circle tightens. No way out
but kick and punch and run,

run at the circle that is receding,
bending under his weight when they collide
a watchface a waterglass something
the size of the sun.
Run, because there is never any finish
run alone   until the circle
becomes the earth around him.

Long-Distance Runner

After the first two miles there is only a body
running upon hard earth past irrelevant trees,
watchful of nothing, attending to its own breathing,
eyes empty and chill as metal, thought released.

Nothing persists but persistence. Though there may be
a curlew whistling, a dog in a frost-grey yard,
a ploughman giddy with gulls, cries from the distance,
vermilion blurs of roofs by the far faint road

over against the canal or sidling the airfield's
windy desolation, and, elsewhere, friends
lovers, children, none of these things can matter;
only the body matters, the mindless blind

insistent throat of air, the compulsive lungbeat,
habitual muscles travelling the steady jolt
and pound of hard-packed by-ways; time only matters
for its obstinate pace by pace retreat,

its grudging admiration of an endurance
pure enough to depend on no profound
intent or oracle, thinking it sufficient
to concentrate on covering the ground.

The Runners

As I strolled the seawall
in the rain, clouds low
above the inlet,
three men jogged past me with such an effortless stride
I suddenly took up their pace
behind them. I don't think they
were a lot younger than me
or older, but they stepped easily
through the downpour,
large-bodied, talking in a friendly manner
to each other. They didn't seem to mind
me joining them, called back
greetings and a few questions
about the weather
as we pounded along, skirting puddles
and dodging umbrellaed walkers
on the path. I knew I was in no shape
for this, but remembered people's opinions
that mine are runner's legs, and continued
yet saved my breath rather than
say much to the others.
I had no idea
where we were running to,
they with their wide shoulders
and confident stride
but I felt no matter what obstacles
or quest we faced
if anyone could win
it was men like these.
Or maybe we were running for nothing,
splashing through the afternoon rain
only to run. And soon I
was too busy keeping my body with them
to care about where we were going.

Climbers

Above the last squeal of wheels
dead-end of the highest road
lithe climbers escape leaping
through fir where chipmunks whirl
Twilight swirls at their backs
magenta hills dissolve
in faces   they curl in crypts
where stone has shelled
and doze while spires snuff out

At dawn along cherry cliffs they stalk
glimpse the peak   on a muskmelon sky
but when glaciers wake chewing
their cud of rock over striped walls
by beryl lakes climbers must shrink
to beetles on brightness   leave birdsong
to follow the spoor of goat over
blocking ramparts by chalky waters

At noon stentorian icegalls call
and hushed they move from the barred old
snow   blindly crawl to cliff's cold
comfort   up up the horny neck of desolation
till their hands bleed at last
from the spines of the crest and they lie
at the end of thrust
weak in weak air and a daze of sight
on the pointless point of the peak

And this is the beginning of space
where there is nothing to say
and no time
except to clamber down down to the road
and the long pigs of the cars squealing

Three Years from Long Beach

in memory, W.J.M., 1964-1987

Westward, till all are drowned, those Lemmings go. — John Masefield

1
Another decade has risen from the east
& still I am dreaming of bears.
In my sleep the devil of your imagining,
cones of teeth & a greatcoat like an old Russian's,
lumbers behind us in a sunbright tunnel of rainforest.

Mornings, I return beyond the black mass
of your dying on the highway later that summer
to what is mine, *that* moment on the path,
chips of cedar & the blanket I summon
of a bear, trope to eclipse the glare

of what I lack. Like acrobats you & I balanced
a score of backward steps on the mulch,
rounding a bend in his sightline
just as *ursa* minced away, each down-
step of the great paws into the foliage

as delicate as a mime's hands. Shadowed
then, the bear expanded to fill the unconscious
of everything. On all sides the ferns rustled
with a commotion of wildlife as we jogged
to the road's shoulder, our heads

swiveling. At the car I juggled keys
by the door. Safe in the driver's seat, I ogled you
through the passenger window, & shrugged
& hesitated, as ever, to let you in.
Perform for me first. Offer me a love

to lock out. So you grinned. You knocked,
mocked horror, smeared your face
into the glass — an agony of compressed features, stretched
lips. You ducked & vanished, the window blank
in the evaporation of your kiss.

2
Rhetoric for grieving: an apparition like this
could torment a man into traffic. In the story I tell
I fumble with keys, attendant to the sacrifice
you banished me from. From across the hardtop
you pray for speed of passage. You sweat, chant,

you play the intoxicate shaman of fear. Demons,
fire on night's freeway, Christ's headlights.
Hallucination: the key snaps off, an arrowhead
in the lock's heart. You see transfiguration:
the galloping bear overcomes you,

Ford Bronco
mauls you on the Trans-Canada:
indents your forehead, crushes your chest;
unfolds a grizzly length, his head to assess me;
is consumed by a forest recess.

3
The white mists are huge on Long Beach. One errs
to seek Japan in the distance. Just westward
of the actually seen, seals & orcas
make pulp of themselves on the crags
of an island, mossalive patch of turf

where the lemming king, fellow
of infinite jest, amuses a citizenry
of sheep
with his eternal prank.
Leaping from a cliff's edge

he lights safe on a high ledge.
His punishment: no gesture is definitive.
(The White myths are huge
on Long Beach. Lies like a landscape
& narrative is the safest place I know.)

4
The next day, on Florencia Bay, cradled by cliffs
too steep for bear feet, I bathed
in a tidal pool's heat; probed
the fingers & the sphincter
of a sticky green anemone; you watched

as I slid into sleep. Floating in litres
of *riesling* I wakened alone, pissing, raw
with salts. Against me the sand rippled
harder than a bodybuilder's tummy & you
had receded, mirage

in a leather jacket, sucking your stone
of hashish & tracking yourself one mile
down the tide. Later, the north Pacific squeezed

an ache into the bones of our calves
as we tested the waters, waded, then

pogoed to avoid the rhythmical
onslaught of froth. We chattered with blue lips
about scrotums, shrunken to snakehide
& cupped in our hands as we hugged
our own chests in our arms —

5

You splash my dry shoulders & the heart
recoils. When you dive, a perfect arc, you never crack
the water: you fall forever, meteoric.
Submerged too, I feel the icy spike in our foreheads.
But there are no trident-tough or musseled

gods under here, barnacled or weed-whipped.
No dashboard figurines with halogen eyes.
Today, I hold you responsible for the duffer's
symbology of your bad trip. But I could regret
not drowning together. Ask anyone:

I have wrecked myself these three years,
so biblical. Since my unsuccessful wisdom-
tooth surgery & your death, I have lost
the power to smile. The ache a numbness,
the numbness lead, I'm anesthetic, unreactive,

sinking with the ebb, my dead-fish
arms, blood cold-dense, I fall from of all
sure footing & my lips will not be said —
so I swallow salt, capsuled kelp,
to see what vitamins they bring,

or dream I'm drowsing in my pool
tanning under an angel's rings,
till tendrils trickle down my throat
& bleach the driftwood of my lungs
a searing sting that sings & sings

6

but still I am not dead. The sea spits
me out & we crawl back to the cabin.
Chill marrow, I bathe again, shivering still
in waves. Waiting for a certain warmth
to penetrate. You slip between my lips

that polished tokestone, urging
pangs to my bronchi from your perch
on the cornice of the tub. Beneath you
I am a nakedness, spread upon the waters.
This loam we inhale, homey as oatmeal,

chewy with tar. Later, on the twin
mattress that is mine, I will attain
the ecstasy of a sleep that comes. Beneath you,
I am a nakedness that cannot touch
or be touched. Always you said, *Once*

with a man, & to me that sounded
like an *idea*. To love in that room
with open doors, to admit the bears, awkward men
no hairier than myself, & to confess
wet dreams at noontide. To live out

on the mainland of my life
these teases, or the sleep-vision that visits me
on your first anniversary:
You are unbroken. Your pocked cheeks
porcelain-clear, my Pierrot

doll. Your pale blue eyes. We meet again
as skins in the ocean, muscles
slick with contact in a goodbye without
talk. For the first time in a decade
I wake up crying, the tang of blood on my tongue

7

& a shooting star in the dawn-grey window.
On the final morning we spiral
cross-Island to Nanaimo. Gusts
of Alberni, sour milltown
on the fjord, waft & wince us

past the motel whose draft we tasted
three nights before, the pub where
woodworkers in Daytons, Macs & black
T-shirts rolled up their poor Player's
& tattooed the floorboards

while an imitation Boss
stomped his nothing hours
across the stage. Glory days.
But this time we pass on, past
another wasted room, past

the ballsy goats of Coombs
to the songs you never stop singing —
Phil Ochs & the country ballads
that soothe my paws on the wheel
till the clatter of the ramp subsides

& we bob in the sooty womb
of the Queen of New Westminster.
The engine ticks as it cools.
All the animals I am, & am running from.
Blame me for something, bastard.

8

For days together we were boys again.
Going home, our ferry riffled the Strait, its
searchlight boring a tunnel through fog
& real Gulf Islands, toward the city's aurora.
Do you, who are memory, remember?

No — you watched me watching your languor
& would not take me in. Even the smoke
you only pretended to ingest, only
by mouth, & with each pass
you wiped my spit from the stone.

But I am between your teeth & palette now.
I am that trickle down your throat
& I enter you, enter you at every avenue.
You like stories? Well this is the baby
you must bear, & must devour, without ending:

We kneel on the prow of a ship
& the wind drags tears from your eyes.
Months from today — you want me to warn you,
you want reasons or signs —
in some nightmare, mad as acid,

I will embrace the highbeams
of a Saskatchewan night:
my perfect trajectory, like a vaudevillian,
from the ditch to a twin spotlight. Just
a flash, but so unpredicted, the news first

will strike you as a hoax. You will spend time
hooking for my pantleg, looking for excuses
on the outside. O — you will need stretches of time
to wrap your hide around
the fact of your absence, & the hard growth of mine.

9
Chameleon tongue, the landspit
of the Tsawwassen dock
swallows us whole into the living continent;
& our lights cut a widening swath
through the darkness on the highway ahead.

Vancouver 1990

Rock Climbing

I
If I could hang on the Niagara Escarpment forever
then I would be a pendulum,
a hanged man or a barometer, emerging in time
to the weather and the hours.
I would be a sign to people; useful as a spoon,
an instrument of calculation: the failed climber.

In my blue rock-helmet and orange harness
I wouldn't spook children, like the dead pilot
in *Lord of the Flies*; I would be orderly and dry,
shucked of thoughts like the moulting falcon in the zoo.
I wouldn't have fallen out of a war, but just stupidity,

being on the wrong step at the worst time. My feet
would have shot out and debris come down after me
perhaps for twenty feet. And when I stopped it would be
with a jolt on the end of the rope like a card at last
in the right slot. I would swing suspended

from my old faithful piton, growing to love it more
with the years. My rope would always invite ascent;
I would ignore it, occupied with circulation and
birches, regarding it as I would a drying umbilical cord,
a telephone wire gone dead.

II
But it is the rope itself
full of lunatic assertions
that electrifies the hanger-on with the insistence
of a heart-attack;
there is always the hope this world
might be less normal than it appeared;
these slow considerations have changed my heavy head.
Hand over hand I am
getting you on the end of the line.
Hello, you fast talker.
Guess who this is.

SID MARTY

The Argument for Ascending

Sidehill gouging
gives your ankles pain
stiffkneed evenings
and arthritic old age

Slabrock and ice
have let so many down
from an awkward balance
in their finger ends
The mystery of falling

Gravity too, is my domain
It turns you, swimmer, over
I watch from the steep approaches

Would you be the man for the mountain?
The skulls of goats, the skulls of sheep
   foot my precipitous fences

Learn to fail sometimes, bear with me

   Your body is the cross you carry
up to the high places

And your reward
a tearing wind
a view

of endless higher mountains

Lilienthal's Glider

When Lilienthal
climbed the sky
he was fully equipped for mountaineering
a jersey and black boots
stockings tucked in
for the rush of alpine air
and then the aureole
of linen and willow
billowing at a heavenly angle
the scientific balance
of wind and velocity
and the precise frame
to arrest the world
But who could predict
the moth with the man dangling
could be
arraigned
the calculating eyes
brought to trial
Lilienthal   beard breaking flame
called into question the essential elements
and when the scientific commandments
became alleluias
they found him
down from the mountain
crumpled in his shower of delicate wings
and no one could tell for sure
that science was still intact
or that the boots and jersey
were a perfect choice
for an aerial voyage.

R. G. EVERSON

Abandoning the Snow

Skiing in the moonlight below zero
we were sad because we had agreed
to go to Texas   Lorna and I had promised
to leave our rented cottage that had no cellar
or any furnace   It had one fireplace
Frost white-bearded on the inside walls,
our cottage was almost too cold for moles
that lived in a corner of the hard dirt floor
We sadly skied across the frozen lake
but we were young and slowly shook off sorrow —
south of Niagara on the way toward Texas
abandoning our fragile Christmas snow

The Song of the Ski

Norse am I when the first snow falls;
Norse am I till the ice departs.
The fare for which my spirit calls
Is blood from a hundred viking-hearts.

The curved wind wraps me like a cloak;
The pines blow out their ghostly smoke.
I'm high on the hill and ready to go —
A wingless bird in a world of snow:
Yet I'll ride the air
With a dauntless dare
That only a child of the north can know.

The bravest ski has a cautious heart
And moves like a tortoise at the start,
But when it tastes the tang of the air
It leaps away like a frightened hare.
The day is gloomy, the curtains half-drawn,
And light is stunted as at the dawn;
But my foot is sure and my arm is brawn.

I poise on the hill and I wave adieu
(My curving skis are firm and true)
The slim wood quickens, the air takes fire
And sings to me like a gypsy's lyre.
Swifter and swifter grows my light:
The dark pines ease the unending white.
The lean, cold birches, as I go by,
Are like blurred etchings against the sky.

One am I for a moment's joy
With the falling star and the plunging bird.
The world is swift as an Arab boy;
The world is sweet as a woman's word.
Never came such a pure delight
To a bacchanal or a sybarite:
Swifter and swifter grows my flight,
And glad am I, as I near the leap,
That the snow is fresh and the banks are deep.

Swifter and swifter on I fare,
And soon I'll float with the birds on air.
The speed is blinding; I'm over the ridge,
Spanning space on a phantom bridge,
The drifts await me; I float, I fall:
The world leaps like a lunging carp.
I land erect and the tired winds drawl
A lazy rune on a broken harp.

T-bar

Relentless, black on white, the cable runs
through metal arches up the mountain side.
At intervals giant pickaxes are hung
on long hydraulic springs. The skiers ride
propped by the axehead, twin automatons
supported by its handle, one each side.

In twos they move slow motion up the steep
incision in the mountain. Climb. Climb.
Somnambulists, bolt upright in their sleep
their phantom poles swung lazily behind,
while to the right, the empty T-bars keep
in mute descent, slow monstrous jigging time.

Captive the skiers now and innocent,
wards of eternity, each pair alone.
They mount the easy vertical ascent,
pass through successive arches, bride and groom,
as through successive naves, are newly wed
participants in some recurring dream.

So do they move forever. Clocks are broken.
In zones of silence they grow tall and slow,
inanimate dreamers, mild and gentle-spoken
blood-brothers of the haemophilic snow
until the summit breaks and they awaken
imagos from the stricture of the tow.

Jerked from her chrysalis the sleeping bride
suffers too sudden freedom like a pain.
The dreaming bridegroom severed from her side
singles her out, the old wound aches again.
Uncertain, lost, upon a wintry height
these two, not separate, but no longer one.

Now clocks begin to peck and sing. The slow
extended minute like a rubber band
contracts to catapult them through the snow
in tandem trajectory while behind
etching the sky-line, obdurate and slow
the spastic T-bars pivot and descend.

Landscape

The snow fell slowly over the long sweep
Of mountain, without aim,
Direction or purpose; at the wind's whim,
The snow came.
Presently over the cool cotton blanket
There was a sound,
A movement on the upper mountain:
A woman's hair unbound,
And falling over white shoulders;
Swerving swift and slow,
The men with winged feet etching intricate
Patterns in the snow.
And presently the light went out, the sun
Dwindled behind a peak and died.
Inside the trees, a wolf or the ghost of a child
Stirred briefly and cried.
Moon-shine turned over shadows and formed
Other shadows, mannikins moved
When a tree moved; and the wind
Carefully erased the grooved
Trail the skiers made. And again,
The rustle of wings in the night.
And again the smooth white
Cup of brightness on the mountain; and man
Far in his outpost cities slept. The moon
Peered between the trees in a slow
Deliberate dance; and paused dramatically
At the barricades, and turned to go
With a soft flow of silver on the planet's edge:
Snow and the threat of snow. . . .

MONTY REID

Cross-Country

because it is warmer than you
thought and you brought the
wrong wax and overdressed

and because it was the first time
out this season and you
haven't kept in shape

and your boots felt stiff
and your breath hurt and your
arms were sore from holding

you up so often.   because
the kids went by you
uphill.   because skidoos

which you still hear
snarling in the valley
chewed the trail up, tho signs

were posted to keep them
out.   because the air
is crystal, the chickadee

you stopped to watch, or
so you explained it,
circled the dry

trunk, head
in the bark, eyes hard with light.
because

there is a need for exercise,
beauty, the heart
nothing but itself,

its urgency, circling,
the skiers across the valley
stride evenly

Water Skier

Evening on Greig Lake
is a sudden shattered sunburst.

The water skier — sorcerer
peels a layer of glass
and hurls it at the dropping sun.

SUSAN M[c]MASTER

Learning to Ride

This, then
to let go,
let the body
move the hands,
drag the brain
without holding on
to words, language,
the ways I've learned
so well to define
and subdue
the twang of nerve ends,
pulse of arteries,
clench and release
of the bundles of fiber
I name to myself *muscle*,
as if the word alone
brings into being
the smooth working humps
under unregarded skin
that carry me,
have carried me
through every single day
unnoticed, till now —

Before I entered this
curious new world
of body direct
it was naming alone
that stood for all else,
the flap of the tongue,
labile and strong,
the only muscular motion
I'd learned to control.
Held thus, at tongue's length,
the world made sense,
a black and white tale
patterned in words
I could stand back to read.
Tear them up, pull them away,
rip them into tendrils
coiling underfoot
and find —

A steady pulsing region
of thick grounded motion,
a shadowed wildland
of caverns, valleys,
always changing footing,

where I move like a tracker
from childhood tales,
like a cat
like a deer,
to the beat of tissues
flex of sinews
spring of limbs
loose, aware,
learning to learn
a whole new language,
of heat and sweat
power and flow
of pushing the body
till it trembles, groans,
learning to discard
the ancient metaphors
of love and soul
and existential pain,
for the uncoded strophes
of pulse and breath

Learning to ride
the muscular heart
the solid bone

So the mind learns to fly
to match the heart's leap
so the heart soars at last
across the mind's divide

After All That

for Jennifer MacKenzie, 17 years old

It is the echo of a streetlight in the window,
blue hat of light.
It is the jeopardy makes me write down.
Like Lazarus, I am raised from the dead.
So many times & never weary.

It is my lungs make me feel this.
The pain the vein spoke when they pushed intravenous into me,
the surprise.
Lazarus too, surprised to have a body
after all that.

You whom we pray to, governors
of the human, of the reported blameless soul.
White-clad people of the hospital.
For *Jennifer MacKenzie*, thrown from a horse

& carried in from air ambulances as I lay there;
unconscious, not breathing on her own;
behind a yellow curtain washed each day & hung between us

You who will never know me, I am sorry.
I'm not blameless.
You whom the medicine won't bring home to your father's sobbing,
I tip my hat of blue light to you, it is silent, a rosary,
it is all I have

The Speed of Falling Bodies

In the public forest, in rain,
the tread of his mountain bike
bites crosswise into a root
& against the grain
of motion. The blur, the running hologram
of foliage is broken, it dangles
off the reel, & the gravel path
approaches his eye
from high-res & curious angles —

— A rush of pebbles
ushers the gouge of one pedal
into the mulch: a scourge
of contact, knee & shoulder
compact with the soil
in an ecstasy of injury
without mystery, the torquing
jolt of clavicle
& the bloody plush of his patella
as vigorous as Sylvia's thumb-cut.

He loves this:
the underside of ferns
soft-tufted in his silence
& dripping. After years
of intravenous, death
by microscope,
the slow pulse
of diffusion into the bath,
bad news by phone
& so many dead
friends per second, this
is fresh, this is life's law
& not senseless. As with

the simple hurts of boyhood
his body weeps
through shredded lycra, sticky
with platelets, while
flat out in the needles
& pillowed by a wheel
he revels
beneath conifers & cloud
in these rich, deep, gorged, gorgeous wounds
that will heal.

Our Boy in Blue

"Edward Hanlan, the most renowned oarsman of any age,
whose victorious career has no parallel in the annals of sport"
— engraved on the statue to Ned Hanlan, CNE grounds, Toronto.

Heroes are usually forgotten
so quickly it says much
for our shallow, fickle minds.

Take Ned Hanlan,
Toronto boy, five-foot-eight,
one hundred fifty pounds,
world-champion oarsman at 25 (1880).
finished at 30, and still
the fastest sculler ever.
Loser of only six races
out of three hundred fifty,
so good he made fools
of nearly all his opponents,
his rowing so smooth,
his sliding so methodical
and free from effort, man and boat
at one with the water.

And yet after five years
he could hardly win a race,
his challenges drew no takers,
And he became hotel-keeper,
then City alderman,
dying young in 1908.

But 20,000 people
filed past his coffin,
and years later they built him
a twenty-foot statue,
where he still stands today,
gazing over Lake Ontario
(where he grew up as a boy,
learned to row
almost as soon as he walked),

perhaps waiting there to see
if some young hopeful
in a single scull will show
inside the breakwater,
stroking hard in dark blue
singlet and vest,
the early-morning sun
glinting back from his oars —

another Boy in Blue?

A SPORTING LIFE

Something about playing outdoors
in the long summer evenings ...
— Bronwen Wallace

Dancing on the Machine

After two years of thralldom to the StairMaster, the Master of Stairs,
the rack with a name straight out of S/M or D&D
two years to climb program by program, each with its twelve
stations of hardship (twelve being the perfect rational number
for self-improvement)
two years of ascending one CN Tower four days per week with
Prince in your ears (*cream, get on top*) or Springsteen (*i'm goin' down*) & every increment an agony, every LED beep of increase
a most proximate approach to your heaving death —

Yes, after two years in bondage to the ecstatic moment, when
the chug for breath, vise of rib & piston's thrust of thigh gives
real meaning to the phrase *burn calories* (your glucose fuel boils
off & you can actually *feel* the fat oxidize, you are so hot your
forearms are sweating & the vapour that emanates starts to smell
a little different, acrid, like smoke) —

Then, after these millions of steps, *only then* are you dancing on the
tops of clouds faster than a running back through old tires
only then have you grimaced your way through an epic rising
narrative to the twelfth chapter of the highest ordained form
only, *today*, do you find it easy, you could laugh at this machine,
razz its microchips & hydraulic pads, its black rubber executioner's
masking, you could just laugh, man, because your graven calves
(that idol's groove in the lateral bulge), your quad-ingots & lithe
feet, steel-belted glutes & the low back you cured this way, oh
this whole lubed mechanism could pump the joints at your knees
forever now, like Ali you are not struggling or practicing a craft
but just dancing

dancing in your prodigious mockery of the man in the mirror, you
give a little kick with every funk embellishment in the Prince track
because you can, because you have extra, but mainly because the
cruel futurist masterpiece has surrendered to you its essence, like
the scientist in *The Fly* you've melded with the jet metal of your
obsession & you are dancing together, salt fluids bind you in an
exchange of properties, the machine takes on flesh & the flesh
machine, you & your Master let go of all enmity, you entwine
your stiff tubular arms & hold one another dear in the grinding
unsyncopated clutch of two immaculate creations in love.

The Game

Don't bother me I'm terribly busy

A child is starting to build a village
It's a city, a county
And who knows
Soon the universe.

He's playing

These wooden blocks are houses he moves about
and castles
This board is the sign of a sloping roof
not at all bad to look at
It's no small thing to know the place where the
road of cards
will turn
This could change completely
the course of the river
Because of the bridge which makes so beautiful a
reflection
on the water of the carpet
It's easy to have a tall tree
And to put a mountain underneath
so it'll be high up

Joy of playing! Paradise of liberties!
But above all don't put your foot in the room
One never knows what might be in this corner
Or whether you are not going to crush the
favourite
among the invisible flowers

This is my box of toys
Full of words for weaving marvellous patterns
For uniting separating matching
Now the unfolding of the dance
And soon a clear burst of the laughter
That one thought had been lost

A gentle flip of the finger
And the star
Which hung carelessly
At the end of too flimsy a thread of light
Falls and makes rings in the water.

Of love and tenderness who would dare to doubt
But not two cents of respect for the established
order

Or for politeness and this precious discipline
A levity and practices fit to scandalize grown-up
  people

He arranges words for you as if they were simple
  songs
And in his eyes one can read his mischievous
  pleasure
At knowing that under the words he moves
  everything about
And plays with the mountains
As if they were his very own.
He turns the room upside down and truly we've
  lost our way
As if it was fun just to fool people.

And yet in his left eye when the right is smiling
A supernatural importance is imparted to the
  leaf of a tree
As if this could be of great significance
Had as much weight in his scales
As the war of Ethiopia
In England's.

We are not book-keepers

Everyone can see a green dollar bill
But who can see through it
          except a child
Who like him can see through it with full freedom
Without being in the least hampered by it
          or its limitations
Or by its value of exactly one dollar

For he sees through this window thousands of
  marvellous toys
And has no wish to choose between these
  treasures
Nor desire nor necessity
Not he
For his eyes are wide open to take everything.

Male Rage Poem

Feminism, baby, feminism.
This is the anti-feminist poem.
It will get called the anti-
feminist poem. Like it or not.
Dedicated to all my friends who
can't get it up in the night,
accused of having male rage during the
day. This is for the poor buggers.
This is for me and incredible boredom
of arguing about feminism, the right
arguments, the wrong arguments, the
circular argument, the arguments that stem
from one bad affair, from one
bad job, no job — whatever; fill in the
blanks __________ __________, fill in the ways
in which you have been hurt. Then I'll
fill in the blanks, and we'll send rosters
of hurt to each other, mail them, stock
them for the record, to say: *Giorgio Di Cicco*
has been hurt in this way x many times.
We will stock closets of Sarah's hurt,
Barbara's hurt, my hurt, Bobby's hurt.
This is where the poem peters out … oops!— that's
penis mentality, that's patriarchal bullshit,
sexist diction and these line lengths are
male oriented.
    Where did he get so much male rage?
From standing out like a man for a bunch of
years, and being called the dirty word.
"When you are 21 you will become a Man."
Christ! Doomed to enslave women ipso
facto, without even the right training for it.
Shouldn't have wasted ten years playing
baseball; should have practised
whipping, should have practised tying up the
girl next door, giving her cigarette burns …
oops! Male rage again! MALE RAGE — the words ring out —
worse than RING AROUND THE COLLAR, worse than KISSED
THE GIRLS AND MADE THEM CRY, jeesus, male rage
in kindergarten. MALE RAGE. You've got
male rage; I look inside myself and scrounge
for all this male rage. Must be there
somewhere. Must be repressing it. I write poems
faster and faster, therapeutically, to make sure
I get most of the rage out. But someone's
always there to say Male Rage — more Male Rage;
I don't leave the house, working on my male rage.

Things may lighten up. My friends may meet
fine women at a party someday and know
what to say to them, like: "I'm not a Man and
you're not a Woman, but let's have dinner
anyway, let's fuck with our eyes closed and
swap roles for an hour."

I'm tired of being a man.
Of having better opportunities,
better job offers,
too much money.
I'm tired of going to the YMCA and
talking jock in the locker room.
I'm tired of all the poems where
I used the "whore" inadvertently.
I'm tired of having secretaries type out
all my poems for me.
I'm tired of being a man.
I'm tired of being a sexist.
I'm afraid of male rage.
I'm afraid of *my* male rage,
this growing thing, this buddy, this
shadow, this new self, this stranger.
It's there. It's there! How could it have
happened? I ate the right things, said
yes to my mother, thought the good
thoughts.
Doc — give it to me straight.
How long do I have before this male rage
takes over completely?
The rest of your life.
Take it like a man.

Sport

some things you cannot joke about.
like hockey. even the man who will
do your seediest laundry, who is
a better mother than you are, will
turn surly when you laugh about hockey,
its vernacular, the slot and the crease,
the pinch, about shooting the puck
into the net, goalkeeper as prophylactic.
he says he doesn't make fun of things
you like, and, *yes*, you say, guilt puckering
your voice, *that's true*, but to yourself
you add, *only because I don't like anything*
so strange.

and then there is football.
he will hunch defensively in front
of the TV, guarding the remote control
sometimes he will talk back angrily
to the set, you try not to let it
worry you. you look at the same screen
as he does, but it is all just
people smashing into each other, over
and over. you have more in common
with the cat, who reaches a paw up
at the mouse-sized figures, thinks
they are real, although he should
know better by now.

I. The Fitness Class

right away you see you don't fit
in.   your clothes, for instance.
you didn't know there was a dress code,
the tight body suit and belt,
leotards, leg warmers.   there is
another woman wearing an old t-shirt
and cut-offs but she doesn't
come back the next day.
and then you are the wrong weight.
no-one else here is fat, they are
wearing perfect bodies
underneath their perfect outfits.
you thought this was for pudgy people
like you but pudgy people don't fit
into the outfits, of course, it
makes sense.   someone is talking
about shin splints and endorphins,
you don't understand a word of it.
the instructor begins the class.
already you know
you won't pass.

II. Après Aerobics

next morning is a gate
someone has been swinging on all night.
your joints feel like lids of jars
screwed on wrong.   the bathroom mirror
offers you something that has slept
face-down on a radial tire.   outside,
the day is stiff with rain.
but you pour yourself full of caffeine,
winch yourself into your car, wince
back into class.   the music settles
under your skin like a bruise.
every song is half a Hershey bar,
you tell yourself, kick, two, three,
you've got to keep it going
you paid for six weeks this
is what you've got coming.

III. The Class Junkie

Carol feels sorry for you.
I know what it's like, she says,
your first time.   she was,
she tells you in a lowered voice,
once 18 pounds overweight.   you express
the required surprise.   then
she discovered aerobics and her life
changed.   she goes whenever she can.
her husband is very supportive,
last year they had their holidays in town
so she wouldn't have to miss class.
you try to feel superior
but can't.   you can see it
happening to you, taking
over your life, everything
subordinated to cellulite.   you try
to feel superior but can't.

GAIL HARRIS

Jerks

A young man often remains a Jerk for a long time.
Or I should say, a Jerk remains a Jerk, for a Jerk cannot
properly be termed a Young Man. That is not
A common Derogatory Term, such as Jerk is.

The Indianapolis Speedway is a Popular Meeting Place
for Jerks. As is the Studio 54 Discotheque in New York City.
Jerks enjoy an atmosphere of tension and the attitude
of a race. They often forget to attach their helmets
Securely. The sun has set in a Jerk's eyes more than one time.

The number of men on my street at any given moment
multiplied five times and divided by four
Equals all the Jerks I've ever met in a lifetime.
There are fifteen Jerks for every fire-hydrant in New York.
In Chicago, Jerks outweigh the police force.
Five Jerks balanced on top of one another make an interesting
pyramid, but the way to heaven is trickier
Than you'd think
There is a fourteen-hole golfcourse for Jerks in Miami.

There are eighteen-hundred ways to free yourself from a Jerk
and one of them is to squeeze yourself through
A keyhole. Another is to sleep in the cesspool
under the porch.
If you find a Jerk by mistake, just drop him in the nearest
mailbox. The Federal Government always
Has need of Jerks. There is a Jerk in every gentleman.

The Game

The city. Much motion. Noise. Smells by the thousands. It was a large city.

In restaurants, bars, lounges, men in black suits, open collars, in the height of fashion were playing cards.

There were no jacks, queens, kings. On each face-card the face of the player. The games went on and on. Sometimes there were arguments, fights, but the games kept on, the players kept playing.

It was their game. Each was playing his own game. His own way. Yet they were together. Around table after table. Endless. On and on.

Some players were hotter than others. They kept their own scores. Sometimes there was laughter. The cards were changed when they wore out.

RHONA McADAM

Circle Game

It's not just family voices now
chanting over the wire, whispering expectations
in her solitary ear; it's not just her mother's eye
that measures her hand when she brings a new man home.
At the reunion, family pictures were fanned
in the ringed fingers of old classmates
and she was back against the gym wall
waiting to be picked, torn between a sport she didn't play
and not wanting to be last.

She's noticed a recent mannerism that has her twisting
the bare finger at night; sometimes she wakes
to scratched skin, wonders if she was holding on
or tearing off the dreamed circle.

The mirror tells her it's nearly too late, and she finds men
harder to meet, and the ones she does, harder to stand.
But she has things to do, and solitude is a friend
who asks no questions, doesn't call late at night
with a voice like whiskey, wanting to come over,
doesn't need to talk right now
about something she said last week.

She goes her own way, unable to explain her reasons for wanting
her own way; entertains visits from old lovers
that sometimes turn maudlin. It seems everyone needs this
more than she does. She knows she will always be
out of step, the odd one at parties, the one
who knows more than most about dead bolts and tire changes,
prefers to sit with the men when talk turns to pregnancy
but no more at home with football.

A Game

Sitting in our blue room
things assemble as usual
and I know that love
has strange parts

and I am its guardian

the china   the Persian rugs
echo our formal arrangement

the chairs obeying the light
drift down from the ceiling
form with the TV
a perfect triangle

I worshipping your
artful absorption
of pictured violence

the padded men who
dance out of the TV
weave their circle
pound their leather hooves
into our delicate floors

so my eyes unable to
lock into yours
put you together
with love

enclose you
with magic wishes
counter-circle
to keep us safe

drive back under glass
the horned men
who must remain covered
at all times.

Palm Sunday

I to whom friends come before their trips,
I have so many suitcases

Palm Sunday: The life line, the heart line, the
head line, & the line of fate

Footsteps into the courtyard & back out,
carrying an old-fashioned television, too heavy,
full of tubes

Boxes of flowers grow on my table in the kitchen
under the narrow light, living the edge of
danger, *so little light*

1 out of 3 women, assaulted sexually, in their lives.

Listening to the World Series in 1968, our eyes
dry, Sirhan Sirhan jailed,
Melissa in the back of Grade 8 geography, an earphone
under her hair,
cheering for the Detroit Tigers.

All of us
remember
some of
some thing

or we wouldn't be here.

We scrub & scrub our rooftops, trying to please.
Please be clean. Please clean me.

Please please me, sang the top rock group with the
same haircut, we traded gum cards of their faces
on the front lawn in the hot summer green of

1965.

In the picture, my brother sits on the front step, small,
wearing the green nylon jacket passed down from the rest of us,
smiling concretely.

1 out of 3 women assaulted.
The locks changed & the windows impregnable.

The Word "impregnable".
What are we saying.
(Impossible) to theorize about the real.

To A Sad Daughter

All night long the hockey pictures
gaze down at you
sleeping in your tracksuit.
Belligerent goalies are your ideal.
Threats of being traded
cuts and wounds
— all this pleases you.
O my god! you say at breakfast
reading the sports page over the Alpen
as another player breaks his ankle
or assaults the coach.

When I thought of daughters
I wasn't expecting this
but I like this more.
I like all your faults
even your purple moods
when you retreat from everyone
to sit in bed under a quilt.
And when I say "like"
I mean of course "love"
but that embarrasses you.
You who feel superior to black and white movies
(coaxed for hours to see *Casablanca*)
though you were moved
by *Creature from the Black Lagoon.*

One day I'll come swimming
beside your ship or someone will
and if you hear the siren
listen to it. For if you close your ears
only nothing happens. You will never change.
I don't care if you risk
your life to angry goalies
creatures with webbed feet.
You can enter their caves and castles
their glass laboratories. Just
don't be fooled by anyone but yourself.

This is the first lecture I've given you.
You're "sweet sixteen" you said.
I'd rather be your closest friend
than your father. I'm not good at advice
you know that, but ride
the ceremonies
until they grow dark.

Sometimes you are so busy
discovering your friends
I ache with a loss
— but that is greed.
and sometimes I've gone
into *my* purple world
and lost you.

One afternoon I stepped
into your room. You were sitting
at the desk where I now write this.
Forsythia outside the window
and sun spilled over you
like a thick yellow miracle
as if another planet
was coaxing you out of the house
— all those possible worlds! —
and you, meanwhile, busy with mathematics.

I cannot look at forsythia now
without loss, or joy for you.
You step delicately
into the wild world
and your real prize will be
the frantic search.
Want everything. If you break
break going out not in.
How you live your life I don't care
but I'll sell my arms for you,
hold your secrets forever.

If I speak of death
which you fear now, greatly,
it is without answers,
except that each
one we know is
in our blood.
Don't recall graves.
Memory is permanent.
Remember the afternoon's
yellow suburban annunciation.
Your goalie
in his frightening mask
dreams perhaps
of gentleness.

AUDREY POETKER

touching home

sprinting along side of you
holding back against
the wind   letting you run
strong   head high
into the sweet summer
the grass is too high
field mice run & grasshoppers
pop like corn
down our path

& if you won
it was no sacrifice
but sacrament
in the days when you touching home
& me touching you
meant safe

susie is here
to complete our trinity
of youth   standing
on each other's shoulders
so high we see eternity
from the tire tied
to the old maple
by the lilac bushes

i remember brownie barking
the world tilting
at our laughter
at onkel john's laugh booming
out from the kitchen

now in your garden
of celestial calm
how infantile i must seem
to you   sister
writing & genuflecting
at each lash of wind
but it's not so much
the words as that each
one finds a grief
to centre on
let's loose a string
of vowels around our necks
& speak of whales & seals
& how we liked to swing

when we were young
& in the raised crosses
& stone tablets
chisel the haiku

of our names

Big Field

Who will read this? Many of them are dead.
The white Pavilion on Big Field is gone,
and everything is altered but the heart
I hurt myself with; even the Drome is done,
ploughed-up, forgotten. *You've come back to look*
the Old School over, then? They all come back.

Even the tireless dead. A smell of sweat
lives in the changing rooms I crouched in, crying,
with a twisted arm; a smell of piss
drifts through the shrill-voiced bogs; my fingers smearing
dubbin are clagged yellow, gritted, sore;
I take the ball and fall; mud claws my nails,

and masks my jersey. *Stand up! Prove yourself!*
Prove that you're not a girl! He grabbed my towel.
That was during the Spanish Civil War
when everyone backed Franco. Thin and pale,
I was martyred small in a narrow bath
at ten years old. Shame is a kind of death.

He is a Doctor now, firm-voiced, assured
with sicknesses, and not among the dead
who came back huge with uniforms, and told
new dirty stories, and smoked cigarettes
openly in the corridors. On one wall
we kept a map of the fighting. When France fell

that summer I cried, walking to Big Field
to play twelfth man in a match that never ended.
It was a hot drugged day. Europe had stopped.
The Gods had lied, and Glory now pretended
that it hadn't meant it. Dreams went sick.
Nobody ever let me get to the wicket;

I stayed in the outfield always. There two boys
taught me the lesser death. The wind is cold
across Big Field, and in the spinney dark
trees gather round dark waters. Long ago
I stood here in my world and felt it crack.
You've come back, then, he said. *They all come back.*

The Game

He answered pools with pebbles, where the sun
hung in its blue void between paving stones
took aim and shattered it; a liquid ridge
of broken stars leapt into space and ran
with shock on shock out almost to the edge
his feet pinned down, then wavered and was gone.
The sun still hung there. He would stand and wait
till it was hard and firm as his two feet,
then bend and scrabble and take aim again.

I stood and watched him answering one pool
all afternoon. I'd thought that it might pall
and he shrug off the game, but it went on,
stone upon stone, as if he kept a rule,
persistently compelled. Above, the sun
hung like a stranger, empty and unreal,
the sky remote. Between his earth-fixed feet
it seemed there hung some question he must meet.
I saw my own sun in another pool.

Commonwealth Games, Edmonton 1978

These lithe figures breezing with ease
through track and field, cycling, the pool,
make my age seem so slow, so unmotivated,
make flesh an ache that grows
with each leg's thrust, arm's release, chest's heave;

and takes me, whether I want to or not,
back to my clumsy days of running, shot-putting,
where the best time of the afternoon's tough work-out
was the warm then cold shower in the musty change-rooms
of Varsity Stadium: where I never ran a race
I didn't end up following another's jersey,
or finishing inches short in the pit. . . .

Which of course made my one victory that much sweeter,
though unbelievable — winning on the High Park slopes
the novice prize of the three-mile UTS cross-country —
me staggering somehow to the finish-line
aware only of great stiffness in both legs,
especially the calves. Then, still almost out of breath,
gulping down hot cocoa at the moment so soothingly welcome
its rancid, burnt taste went unnoticed
until five minutes later I threw up foamy chocolate,
clutching my medal through the ungentlemanly performance.

So today watching winners mount the victory platform,
I'm sure I know how they feel —
ageless, still strong through all their tiredness
with the world grabbed by the tail — (but no taste of cocoa-bile
between their lips, that's left for the second-raters,
and after that the misfits and the old …),

which today these gorgeous bodies have no time, no eye for,
(and fittingly so) — savouring their gold and silver hours!

Red Light, Green Light

Something about playing outdoors
in the long summer evenings after supper
the particular quality of the light then
how it seemed to round
and soften even the most heat-glazed afternoons
so that the memory of those games
— the grace of our bodies emerging from the awkward
tangle of an ordinary growing up
into the fluid movement of our play —
has the glow of a painting
by Christopher Pratt   an adult's dream
of a lost time

The best game was
Red Light   Green Light
the person who was it stood
at the side of the house
back turned against the others
poised at the garden's edge
ready to move
when the call began
green light   green light   green light
moving quietly forward
then   *red light*   and everyone stopped
freezing in mid-step
as the person who was it turned
to catch anyone who moved
I see Sharon   You're it
This was a game we played
only in the evenings   a game that belonged
to that particular light   its way
of gathering the sounds of our playing
into itself

When you were it you could barely
hear the movements of the others
faint rustlings in the air behind you
fainter than your own fading voice
green light   green light   green light
the chant shivering away from you
half afraid to turn and waiting
for someone to spring from behind
grab you by the shoulders
Home Free   You're it again

Something about the way that light
was easing the day so slowly away
from us   the figure huddled
at the side of the house
growing smaller and smaller
as the distance from the garden's edge stretched
ahead until the sounds of our own feet
in the grass seemed to follow us
like invisible animals
and the voices of our mothers
drifted toward us
from another world
impossible to think of entering
the harsh yellow light   the improbable rituals
of toothbrushes and bedtime stories
green light   green light   green light

but even as we kept gliding dreamily
toward that sound
now fragile as the light around us
even then we were changing   stiffened
by our mothers' voices   their shrill
authority making the damp ground suddenly
cold to our bare feet   Sharon!
Right now!   I mean it!   *green light*
green light   Sharon!
the huddled figure turning then
larger for a moment   flash of white
limbs disappearing   the dark shape
of her mother in the porch light
bringing the night down darker
behind us   *g'night*
g'night

Something about that game and the particular
receding light drawing our voices
away with it   our footsteps almost soundless
in the hushed grey grass
as if the act of memory itself
were a kind of moving   a trick
of knowing when to turn and how
the way I walk through a summer's
evening now feeling my body soften
under a loose cotton dress
and the sound of my footsteps
making me turn and stop

and stand there   half surprised
to find myself alone
no other children poised in mid-step
leaning toward me

ACKNOWLEDGEMENTS

Milton Acorn, "The Fights" from *I Shout Love and Other Poems* by Milton Acorn, edited by James Deahl; published by Aya Press, Toronto. Copyright © 1987 by the Estate of Milton Acorn. Originally published in *The Brain's the Target* 1960.

Chuck Angus, "Gordie and My Old Man" from *One Job Town* recorded by the Grievous Angels for Stony Plain Records. Copyright © 1990 by Chuck Angus. Reprinted by permission of Chuck Angus.

David Arnason, "The Joggers" from *Skrag* by David Arnason. Copyright © 1987 by David Arnason. Reprinted by permission of Turnstone Press, Winnipeg.

Margaret Atwood, "Woman Skating" and "Younger Sister, Going Swimming" from *Selected Poems 1966-1984* by Margaret Atwood. Copyright © 1990 by Margaret Atwood. Reprinted by permission of Oxford University Press Canada. Originally published in *Procedures for Underground* by Margaret Atwood.

Margaret Avison, "Tennis" and "The Swimmer's Moment" from *The Dumbfounding* by Margaret Avison. Copyright © 1966 by Margaret Avison. Reprinted by permission of W. W. Norton & Company, Inc.

Earle Birney, "Climbers" from *Ghost in the Wheels* Copyright © 1977 and 1991 by Earle Birney. Reprinted by permission of the Canadian Publishers, McClelland & Stewart, Toronto.

Roo Borson, "Hockey Night in Canada" from *Intent, or the Weight of the World* by Roo Borson; published by McClelland and Stewart. Copyright © 1989 by Roo Borson. Reprinted by permission of Roo Borson.

George Bowering, "Baseball, a poem in the magic number 9," and "Ted Williams" were originally published in *Baseball and Other Poems* by George Bowering; reprinted in *Selected Poems: Particular Accidents* by George Bowering. Copyright © 1980 by George Bowering. "Baseball, a poem in the magic number 9," "Ted Williams" "Exhibition Stadium 1986," "Nat Bailey Stadium 1987," "Oliver Community Park 1948," "Olympic Stadium 1977," and "Parc Jarry 1969" from *Urban Snow*. Copyright © 1992 by Geoge Bowering. All poems reprinted by permission of Talonbooks Ltd., Burnaby, BC.

Kate Braid, "Mother of the Lacrosse Goalie." Printed by permission of Kate Braid.

Alf Brooks, "Plato's Bonspiel." Printed by permission of Alf Brooks.

Kelley Jo Burke, "At the arena" first published in *CVII* volume 14, 1991. Copyright © 1991 by Kelley Jo Burke. Reprinted by permission of Kelley Jo Burke.

Stew Clayton, "The Bonspiel Song" recorded on *Stew Clayton "Country"* by Stew Clayton for Sunshine Records, Winnipeg. Printed by permission of Stew Clayton.

Mark Cochrane, "Boy," "Craft in the Body" and "Daddy is a Monkey" from *Boy Am I*. Copyright © 1995 by Mark Cochrane. Reprinted by permission of Wolsak and Wynn, Toronto. "Three Years from Long Beach" from *32 Degrees*, published by DC Books, Montreal. Copyright © 1993 by Mark Cochrane. "Dancing on the Machine," "High Five," "The Speed of Falling Bodies," "Tear Gas" and "99" and all other poems reprinted by permission of Mark Cochrane.

Dennis Cooley, "Fielding" from *Leaving* Copyright © 1980 by Dennis Cooley. Also reprinted in *Section Lines: A Manitoba Anthology*. Reprinted by permission of Turnstone Press, Winnipeg.

Lorna Crozier, "The Swimmer" from *Inventing the Hawk* by Lorna Crozier. Copyright © 1992 by Lorna Crozier. Reprinted by permission of the Canadian Publishers, McClelland & Stewart, Toronto.

Barry Dempster, "Bases" from *Positions to Pray In* by Barry Dempster. Copyright © 1989 by Barry Dempster. Reprinted by permission of Guernica Press, Toronto.

Pier Giorgio Di Cicco, "Male Rage Poem" from *Flying Deeper into the Century* by Pier Giorgio Di Cicco. Copyright © 1982 by Pier Giorgio Di Cicco. Reprinted by permission of the Canadian Publishers, McClelland & Stewart, Toronto.

H. C. Dillow, "Child Swimming in the Ramapo" first published in *Wascana Review* volume 25, 1990. Copyright © 1990 The University of Regina. Reprinted by permission of *Wascana Review*.

R. G. Everson, "Abandoning the Snow" and "A Real Pro" from *Poems About Me* by R. G Everson. Copyright © by R. G. Everson. Reprinted by permission of Oberon Press, Ottawa.

Judith Fitzgerald, "The Baseball Hall of Fame," "How Do You Spell Relief?" and "Line Drives" from *Diary of Desire* by Judith Fitzgerald. Copyright © 1987 by Judith Fitzgerald. Reprinted by permission of Black Moss Press, Windsor.

Cecelia Frey, "Running" from *The Least You Can Do is Sing* by Cecelia Frey, published by Longspoon Press. Copyright © 1982 by Cecelia Frey. Reprinted by permission of Cecelia Frey.

Leonard Gasparini, "Junk Ball" from *One Bullet Left* by Leonard Gasparini; published by Alive Press, Guelph. Copyright © 1974 by Leonard Gasparini. Reprinted by permission of Leonard Gasparini.

C. H. Gervais, "The Tease of Tiger Town" and "Maggie T Goes Public" from *Public Fantasy* by C. H. Gervais; published by Sequel Press. Copyright © 1983 by C. H. Gervais. Reprinted by permission of C. H. Gervais.

Leona Gom, "II. Après Aerobics," "III. The Class Junkie," "I. The Fitness Class" and "Sport" from *Private Properties* by Leona Gom, 1986; reprinted in *The Collected Poems*, 1991. Copyright © by Leona Gom. Reprinted by permission of Sono Nis Press, Victoria.

Grande, Troni Y., "For Antigone, Excluded from Sand-Volleyball" by Troni Y. Grande, reprinted from *CVII*, volume 15, 1993.

Don Gutteridge, "Arena," "Running (and Ground)," "Skating," and "Shooting" from *A True History of Lambton County* by Don Gutteridge. Copyright © 1977 by Don Gutteridge. Reprinted by permission of Oberon Press, Ottawa.

Gail Harris, "Jerks" from *Poets 88* edited by Ken Norris and Bob Hilderley. Copyright © 1988 by Gail Harris. Reprinted by permission of Quarry Press, Kingston.

Richard Harrison, "The African Hockey Poems, 1 and 2," "Coach's Corner," "The Feminine," "On the American Express Ad Photo of Cardmembers Gordie Howe and Wayne Gretzky Talking After the Game" and "Rhéaume" from *Hero of the Play* by Richard Harrison. Copyright © 1994 by Richard Harrison. Reprinted by permission of Wolsak and Wynn, Toronto.

Steven Heighton, "Endurance" from *Poets 88* edited by Ken Norris and Bob Hilderley. Copyright © 1988 by Steven Heighton. Reprinted by permission of Quarry Press, Kingston.

David Helwig, "Stopping on Ice" from *The Rain Falls Like Rain* by David Helwig. Originally published in *The Best Name of Silence*, 1972. Copyright © 1982 by David Helwig. Reprinted by permission of Oberon Press, Ottawa.

John Frederic Herbin, "The Diver" from *Marshlands* by John Frederic Herbin. Copyright © John Frederic Herbin. Published by The Ryerson Press, Toronto.

Susan Ioannou, "Golf Lesson" first published in *CVII* volume 15, 1993; revised and reprinted in *Where the Light Waits* by Ekstasis Editions, Victoria. Copyright © 1996 by Susan Ioannou. Reprinted by permission of Susan Ioannou.

Paulette Jiles, "Rock Climbing" from *Celestial Navigation* by Paulette Jiles; published by McClelland and Stewart, Toronto. Copyright © 1984 by Paulette Jiles. Reprinted by permission of Paulette Jiles.

Lionel Kearns, "Hockey is Zen" from *This is a Poem*, edited by Florence McNeil, first published in *Ignoring The Bomb* by Oolichan Press, Lantzville. Copyright © 1982 by Lionel Kearns. Reprinted by permission of Lionel Kearns.

A. M. Klein, "Lone Bather" and "Wrestling Ring" from *The Rocking Chair and Other Poems* by A. M. Klein, and *Collected Works of A. M. Klein* by A. M. Klein, edited by Zailig Pollock. Copyright © 1948 and 1990 by A. M. Klein. Reprinted by permission of University of Toronto Press.

August Kleinzahler, "Boxing On Europe's Most Beautiful Beach" and "Sundown at Fletcher's Field" from *Storm Over Hackensack* by August Kleinzahler. Copyright © 1985 by August Kleinzahler. Published by Moyer Bell. Reprinted by permission of Moyer Bell. "Winter Ball" from *Red Sauce, Whiskey and Snow* by August Kleinzahler. Copyright © 1995 by August Kleinzahler. Published by Farrar, Straus & Giroux. Reprinted by permission of Farrar, Straus & Giroux.

Robert Kroetsch, "The Bridegroom Rises to Speak," "Four Questions for George Bowering," "Listening to the Radio: For Michael Ondaatje," "Reading It in the (Comic) Papers: For bp," "Philosophy of Composition: For Paul Thompson" and "Wedding Dance, Country-Style" from *Completed Field Notes* by Robert Kroetsch; published by McClelland & Stewart, Toronto. Copyright © 1989 by Robert Kroetsch. Reprinted by permission of Robert Kroetsch.

Irving Layton, "The Breaststroke," "Golfers," and "The Swimmer" from *A Wild Peculiar Joy* by Irving Layton. Copyright © 1989 by Irving Layton. Reprinted by permission of the Canadian Publishers, McClelland & Stewart, Toronto.

John B. Lee, "Falstaff as a Hockey Goalie: taking the Edge off," "The Hockey Player Sonnets," "Industrial League Hockey," "Sitting in the Grays by Blues" and "The Trade that Shook the Hockey World" from *The Hockey Player Sonnets* by John B. Lee. Copyright © 1991 by John B. Lee. Reprinted by permission of Penumbra Press, Ottawa.

Glynn A. Leyshon, "Above the Jungle Law," "Bil (the throwing dummy)," "Dressing for the Match" and "The Weigh-In." Printed by permission of Glynn A. Leyshon.

Dorothy Livesay, "Soccer Game," from *Collected Poems* by Dorothy Livesay. Copyright © by Dorothy Livesay. Reprinted by permission of Dorothy Livesay.

Douglas Lochhead, "The Game" from *The Panic Field* by Douglas Lochhead. Copyright © 1984 by Douglas Lochhead. Published by Fiddlehead Poetry & Goose Lane Editions, Fredericton. Reprinted by permission of Douglas Lochhead.

Sid Marty, "The Argument for Ascending" from *Headwaters* by Sid Marty. Copyright © by Sid Marty. Reprinted by permission of the Canadian Publishers, McClelland & Stewart, Toronto.

Wilson MacDonald, "The Song of the Ski" reprinted from *Canadian Poetry in English*, B Carman, Lorne Pierce and V. B Rhodenizer, editors, published by The Ryerson Press, Toronto. Copyright © Wilson MacDonald.

Rhona McAdam, "Circle Game" from *The Hour of the Pearl* by Rhona McAdam. Copyright © 1987 by Rhona McAdam. Reprinted by permission of Thistledown Press, Saskatoon.

David McFadden, "107. Hamilton Tiger Cats" from *A Trip Around Lake Huron* by David McFadden; published by Coach House Press, Toronto. Copyright © 1980 by David McFadden. Reprinted by permission of David McFadden.

Don McKay, "Softball" from *Sanding Down this Rocking Chair* by Don McKay; "Taking Your Baby to the Junior Hockey Game" from *Birding or Desire* by Don McKay. Copyright © 1987 and Copyright © 1983 by Don McKay. Reprinted by permission of the Canadian Publishers, McClelland & Stewart, Toronto.

Susan McMaster, "Learning to Ride" from *Learning to Ride* by Susan McMaster. Copyright © 1994 by Susan McMaster. Reprinted by permission of Quarry Press, Kingston.

Florence McNeil, "Family Pond," "First Dive," "A Game," "Half Time Parade," "Hockey," "Lilienthal's Glider," "Meeting of the Animals" and "Skating" from *Ghost Towns* by Florence McNeil; published by McClelland & Stewart. Copyright © 1975 by Florence McNeil. Reprinted by permission of Florence McNeil.

George McWhirter, "Ace," and "Bangor Municipal Golf Course" from *Fire Before Dark* by George McWhirter. Copyright © 1983 by George McWhirter. Reprinted by permission of Oberon Press, Ottawa.

Erin Mouré, "After All That," "The Runner," "Safety" and "A Sporting Life" from *Domestic Fuel.* by Erin Mouré; "Palm Sunday" from *Furious* by Erin Mouré. Copyright © 1985 and Copyright © 1989 by Erin Mouré. Reprinted by permission of Anansi Press and Stoddart Publishing, Don Mills.

Ken Norris, "The Agony of Being an Expos Fan," and "Ode to Baseball" published in *Descant* volume 22, 1991. "Baseball" from *Alphabet of Desire* and "The Failure of Baseball" from *The Music* both by Ken Norris; published by ECW Press, Toronto. Copyright © 1991 and Copyright © 1995 by Ken Norris; "Guy Lafleur and Me" and "The Hawk" from *In the House of No* by Ken Norris; published by Quarry Press, Kingston. Copyright © 1991 by Ken Norris. All poems reprinted by permission of Ken Norris.

Alden Nowlan, "Golf" from *Playing the Jesus Game* by Alden Nowlan. Copyright © 1970 by Alden Nowlan. Reprinted by permission of Claudine Nowlan.

Michael Ondaatje, "Proust in the Waters" and "To A Sad Daughter" from *Secular Love* by Michael Ondaatje; published by Coach House Press, Toronto. Copyright © 1984 by Michael Ondaatje. Reprinted by permission of Michael Ondaatje.

P. K. Page, "T-bar" from *The Metal and the Flower* and *P. K. Page: Poems Selected and New* by P.K. Page; also in *The Oxford Book of Canadian Verse*; published by Oxford University Press, Toronto. Copyright © 1974 by P. K. Page. Reprinted by permission of P. K. Page.

Audrey Poetker, "Touching Home" from *i sing for my dead in german* by Audrey Poetker. Copyright © 1986 by Audrey Poetker. Reprinted by permission of Turnstone Press, Winnipeg.

Thelma Poirier, "Ice Maker" from *Double Vision* by Thelma Poirier and Jean Hillabold. Copyright © 1984 by Thelma Poirier. Reprinted by permission of Coteau Books, Regina.

E. J. Pratt, "Jock o' the Links" from *Collected Poems: Part 1* by E. J. Pratt. Copyright © 1989 by University of Toronto Press. Reprinted by permission of University of Toronto Press.

Al Purdy, "Hockey Players," "Homage to Ree-shard" from *The Collected Poems of Al Purdy.* published by McClelland & Stewart, Toronto. Copyright © 1986 by Al Purdy. "Called on Accounta Rain" and "Landscape" and all other poems reprinted by permission of Al Purdy.

John Reibetanz, "Advice to a Young Skater" first published in *Wascana Review*, volume 27, 1993. Copyright © 1993 The University of Regina. Reprinted by permission of *Wascana Review.*

Monty Reid, "Cross-country" from *The Dream of Snowy Owls* by Monty Reid; published by Longspoon Press. Copyright © 1983 by Monty Reid. Reprinted by permission of Monty Reid.

Brian Richardson, "Night Star Special" from *Reflections from a Basement Window* by Brian Richardson. Copyright © 1983 by Brian Richardson. Reprinted by permission of The Prairie Publishing Co., Winnipeg.

Ken Rivard, "Ice Time," "Reliever" and "Time Has Nothing to Do" from *Kiss Me Down to Size* by Ken Rivard. Copyright © 1983 by Ken Rivard. Reprinted by permission of Thistledown Press, Saskatoon.

Charles G. D. Roberts, "The Skater" from *The Collected Poems of Sir Charles G. D. Roberts: A Critical Edition*; 1901, Wombat Press, Sackville, NS.

Saint-Denys-Garneau, "The Game" translated by F. R. Scott appears in *The Collected Poems of F. R. Scott.* Copyright © 1981 F. R. Scott. Reprinted by permission of the Canadian Publishers, McClelland & Stewart, Toronto. Originally appeared in *Poetry of French Canada in Translation* published by Oxford University Press, Toronto.

Stephen Scriver, "Clearing," "Once is Once Too Many" and "The Way it Was" from *More! All Star Poet* by Stephen Scriver. Copyright © 1981 and Copyright © 1989 by Stephen Scriver. Reprinted by permission of the author and Coteau Books, Regina.

Sandy Shreve, "Surfaces" from *Bewildered Rituals* by Sandy Shreve. Copyright © 1992 by Sandy Shreve. Reprinted by permission of Polestar Book Publishers, Vancouver.

Jane Siberry, "Hockey" recorded on *bound by the beauty* by Jane Siberry. Copyright © 1989 by wing-it/red sky music. Reprinted by permission of Bob Blumer and Jane Siberry.

Martin Singleton, "Circle of the Runner," and "Right-handed Hook Shot, 15 Feet Out," from *Difficult Magic* by Martin Singleton. Copyright © 1984 by Martin Singleton. Reprinted by permission of Wolsak and Wynn, Toronto.

Robin Skelton, "Big Field," "The Game" and "Long-Distance Runner" from *The Collected Shorter Poems: 1947-1977* by Robin Skelton; published by Sono Nis Press. Copyright © 1981 by Robin Skelton. Reprinted by permission of Robin Skelton.

David Solway, "The Snorkler" from *Stones in the Water* by David Solway. Copyright © 1983 by David Solway. Reprinted by permission of Mosaic Press, Oakville.

Glen Sorestad, "Water Skier" from *Ancestral Dances* by Glen Sorestad; published by Coteau Press, Regina. Copyright © 1985 by Glen Sorestad. Reprinted by permission of Glen Sorestad.

Raymond Souster, "*Bocce* Players, September," "Christmas-Morning Hockey," "Commonwealth Games, Edmonton 1978," "Jays Win American League East, 1985," "Little Bat At Last Broken," "Marathon Swimmers" and "Our Boy In Blue" from *Collected Poems of Raymond Souster.* Copyright © 1980-1984 by Raymond Souster. Reprinted by permission of Oberon Press, Ottawa.

Birk Sproxton, "The Coach Read the Signs," "The Hockey Fan Hears the Muse," "The Hockey Fan Reflects on Beginnings," "Playing Time Is a Fiction," and "Rules for a Hockey Story" from *The Hockey Fan Came Riding* by Birk Sproxton. Copyright © 1990 by Birk Sproxton. Reprinted by permission of Red Deer College Press, Red Deer.

James Strecker, "Hockey Haiku" from *Bones to Bury* by James Strecker. Copyright © 1984 by James Strecker. Reprinted by permission of Mosaic Press, Oakville.

The Tragically Hip, "Fifty Mission Cap" from the MCA Recording *Fully Completely.* Copyright © by The Tragically Hip. Reprinted by permission of Roll Music/Little Smoke Music.

Alix Vance, "December River Blues." and "Diamond Warrior" first appeared in *The Digby Courier,* July 1990. Copyright © 1990 by Alix Vance. Reprinted by permission of Alix Vance.

Bronwen Wallace, "Red Light, Green Light" from *Signs of the Former Tenant* by Bronwen Wallace. Copyright © 1983 by Bronwen Wallace. Reprinted by permission of Oberon Press, Ottawa.

Miriam Waddington, "Cadenza" from *Collected Poems* by Miriam Waddington. Copyright © 1986 by Miriam Waddington. Reprinted with permission of Oxford University Press Canada, Toronto.

Tom Wayman, "The Runners" from *In a Small House on the Outskirts of Heaven* by Tom Wayman. Copyright © 1989 by Tom Wayman. Reprinted by permission of Harbour Publishing.

Every effort has been made to contact and credit copyright holders for every poem reprinted in this book. If any errors or omissions have occurred, the Editors and Publisher offer our apologies and welcome corrections for subsequent editions of the book.

INDEX BY AUTHOR